The Babysitter Chronicles is published by
Stone Arch Books,
A Capstone Imprint
1710 Roe Crest Drive,
North Mankato, Minnesota 56003
www.mycapstone.com

Cataloging-in-Publication data is available on the Library of Congress website.
ISBN: 978-1-4965-2755-4 (library binding)
ISBN: 978-1-4914-8862-1 (paperback)
ISBN: 978-1-4965-2759-2 (eBook PDF)

Summary: As part of a plan to win back her former best friend, Olivia Bittter agrees to
babysit at a haunted house.

Designer: Veronica Scott
Cover illustration: Tuesday Mourning
Image credits: Anda Marie Photography, pg. 152; Shutterstock: Guz Anna, design element,
Marlenes, design element, Woodhouse, design element, Vector pro, design element

Printed in Canada
102015   009223FRS16

The
BABYSITTER
Chronicles

Olivia Bitter, Spooked-Out Sitter

by Jessica Genderson

STONE ARCH BOOKS
a capstone imprint

Sitter Smarts

Only take jobs you know you can handle.

Chapter 1

"It was a dark and stormy night," I said.

A gust of wind answered, sending a flutter of dead leaves skittering across the sidewalk. I shivered, took a deep breath, and turned the corner. The House loomed ahead. Dark windows, like evil eyes, glared down at me. Gnarled vines clawed the walls like fingers.

"It was a dark and stormy night." I said again, more softly this time. No one answered. I was alone.

"A dark and stormy night" was how my long-time best friend, Beth, and I always started our ghost stories. Whenever we walked past The House (emphasis on each word: *The. House.*), we whispered stories we'd imagined about the ghosts and murderers and creatures and villains who lived within its walls. My stories were scary, but Beth's usually made us giggle, which helped ease our fears when walking past *The. House.*

But today I was alone. Just like every day this week . . . and last week . . . and the week before. Ever since we'd started seventh grade a few months ago, Beth had made up one excuse after another to avoid walking home from school with me.

She'd say, "I'm going to stay after to make posters for Spirit Week," or, "My mom is picking me up and we're going to the mall," or, "I'm going to help Mr. Billings clean up the science room." All excuses, never the truth.

The truth was that Beth was becoming Miss Popular, and I was anything but. She didn't want to be seen with me anymore. She preferred to spend her time with the cool crowd, especially her new best friend, Avery.

Beth and I had been best friends all through elementary school. When we started junior high,

I didn't think anything would change—not about our friendship, anyway. That first day, hundreds of new faces lined the halls and cafeteria, and Beth and I stuck close together. But after that first day, things did change. Beth changed. She wasn't interested in anything we used to do, like watching anime cartoons or making up ghost stories. Now she was only interested in the latest fashions and designer boots.

Beth was really focused on what everyone else was wearing too. She and Avery took turns carrying around a secret notebook. Inside, they wrote down everything all the girls in our class wore every day. Next to each girl's name, they'd draw a smiley face for clothes they liked or a frowny face for clothes they didn't.

How did I know this? Well, one day last week, when Beth reluctantly agreed to come over after school, I peeked at the notebook while she was in the bathroom. Of course, I looked for my name. Frowny faces for every single day. And Beth had even written "Yuck!" next to my manga T-shirt. I was stunned. Beth had always liked that shirt. At least, she'd always said she did.

What upset me the most is Beth knew how much I loved manga comics. She knew my dream was to write my own manga-style series one day. I knew Beth didn't love manga as much as I did (probably no one did), but the fact that she would make fun of it devastated me.

After she left that day, I told my mom I needed new clothes. My mom laughed. "We just bought you a bunch of new clothes for school," she said.

Yeah, a couple new manga T-shirts and a Wonder Woman sweater. I knew I'd get more "Yucks" next to my name if I wore those. "They're not the right clothes," I muttered.

"But you begged for them at the store!" Mom said, frowning in surprise.

I gave her my most convincing stare. "I would like a designer handbag. And suede boots. And a black skater skirt from Nordstrom," I told her. "Like the one Avery wore today."

Mom laughed. "The only way you're getting those is if you buy them yourself."

Myself? How on earth would I ever save up enough money?

Another gust of wind jolted me from my thoughts. I was nearing the block of *The. House.* Even though Beth and I had made up our stories about it, we knew it was definitely haunted. It had been abandoned forever—a crumbly old mansion with turrets and broken windows, an overgrown yard crawling with thorny weeds, and a tall, wrought-iron fence with sharp spires that would poke you you-know-where if you tried to climb over. I wouldn't be surprised if there was even a cemetery in the backyard. No one has lived there for years. *No one could live there,* I heard Beth's voice say in my head. *No one alive, that is. Only ghosts.* And for a split second, I thought I heard her cackling laughter.

And the strangest of them all is the spirit of a little girl, Lillian, I added. Lillian was my favorite ghost. *On a dark and stormy night, Lillian fell down the cellar steps, into a narrow hole. She cried for help, but no one could reach her. She wailed and wailed, and even after she died down there, she kept wailing . . .*

Sometimes her face appears at the window, Beth's voice continued. *And instead of just Boo! she yells, "Bibbledy-bobbledy-boo!"*

I started to laugh, but then I froze. A face appeared at the turret window.

And looked right at me.

And then vanished.

I let out a bloodcurdling scream and started to run. But then something, or someone, grabbed me. I whirled to see a little girl holding on tightly to my jacket. Her skin was so pale I felt I could almost see through it. White-blond, ghostly hair wafted about her head. She stared at me without blinking even once.

Lillian. Lillian the cellar-ghost, right before my eyes.

I tugged my jacket, but she held fast. She let out a strange giggle.

"Let go!" I pleaded.

She shook her head solemnly. "Hi," she whispered. "Do you want to play?"

My heart raced. I closed my eyes. "No, please, no!" I moaned.

The front gate swung open with a clang. I opened my eyes and screamed again. In front of me stood a tall man with wild eyes and messy hair. His face was smeared with dirt. He looked like he'd just crawled from a grave.

"Please don't hurt me," I begged. "I'll do whatever you ask. Just please, don't—"

The man's loud laugh interrupted me. "Hurt you? Why would I hurt you?" he said. "I'm just a friendly neighbor."

"That's what they all say," I muttered. "To lure you in. And then . . ."

"You have quite the imagination!" the man said. He held out a grimy hand for me to shake. I just stared at it.

"Tell Lillian to let go of me," I said. "Please tell her to let go."

The man frowned. "Who's Lillian? This is my daughter Frannie. And I'm Bob Wolf. We just moved in."

"Wolf? Like the animal that bites? And howls at the moon?" I said.

Bob Wolf laughed. "Yes. The Wolfs!" Then he arched his neck and howled, like a wolf would. Lillian/Frannie giggled and howled too.

"Do you want to play?" Lillian/Frannie whispered again, after she'd stopped howling.

Mr. Wolf smiled. "She must like you!" he said to me. "She's usually shy around strangers."

My heart had stopped racing (for the time being), and I was beginning to feel stupid for my scaredy-cat reaction. "You just moved in here?" I asked, nodding toward *The. House.*

Mr. Wolf sighed. "Yes. It's quite the fixer-upper." He shrugged. "But it has a fascinating history. Did you know that—"

"Bob?" a woman's voice called. I looked up to see the face at the turret window. A woman's face. A human face, not a ghost.

"Ah, Mommy's calling us!" Mr. Wolf said to Frannie. He turned to me. "But before we go, what is your name? You never told me."

I hesitated. I still felt a bit wary. "Olivia," I finally said. "Olivia Bitter."

Mr. Wolf raised his eyebrows. "Oh! I believe I met your mother today. She brought over some cookies as a housewarming gift."

"*Mmmm*, good!" Frannie said.

I nodded. "Mom's cookies are to die for," I said, instantly regretting my choice of words. "I mean, they're really good."

"Like I said," Mr. Wolf went on, "Frannie doesn't usually take to strangers. But she likes you, and we're in need of a babysitter next weekend."

"I don't know," I said, looking again at *The. House.*

"Think about it," he said. "Oh, and we have three other kids. There's Robert, who's nine, twin girls Jolene and Josephine, who are seven, and little Frannie here, who's four."

"Um, that's a lot!" I said.

"I know. That's why we pay well."

My mind raced. I hadn't babysat much in my life . . . well, really not at all. But I could really use the money. I had a designer handbag to buy.

"We would need you for the whole weekend," Bob added. "Overnight, too. How old did you say you were?"

"I didn't say," I told him. "I'm thirteen."

Mr. Wolf sighed. "Too young for overnights." He nudged Frannie, who was still gripping my jacket. "Let's go in!"

"Wait!" I said. I glanced up at *The. House.,* then back to Mr. Wolf. I suddenly wanted to see the inside. And if I babysat here, Beth would definitely want to see the inside too. I could win her back. And I'd have cash to buy boots that would rival Avery's any day.

"My mom could help with the overnights," I told him. "I'm old enough to sit during the day."

"Bob!" the woman's voice called again.

Mr. Wolf nodded. "Have your mom call me," he said. I watched as he and Frannie disappeared inside *The. House.*

I rushed home and burst through the door, yelling "Mom!" Then I remembered she had class today. She owns a yoga studio and teaches yoga classes here and there throughout the week. I would have to wait.

I sat on my bed and paged through my favorite manga series, Shadow City. The series featured Mitsuko—a brainy, serious teenager by day, ultra-cool girl warrior by night. She could take on the hardest Tokyo criminals without breaking a sweat. She wouldn't be at all scared of *The. House.*

When my mom finally got home, I told her about my babysitting offer.

"The Wolfs seem like a nice family," she said. "But do you really think you can handle it?"

"Of course I can handle it!" I said. "It can't be that hard. They're just kids."

Mom looked doubtful. "But overnight? In that house you and Beth are always so scared of?"

"*Were.* We *were* scared," I corrected. "Not anymore. And overnight will be the easiest part. The kids will be asleep. And you'll be there."

A loud crash boomed from the kitchen. I jumped.

"Sorry!" Dad called. "These pots and pans are slippery!"

"You're pretty jumpy," Mom said, eyeing me closely.

I rolled my eyes. "Dad's so loud when he cooks," I said.

"If you get scared at any time, you'll call me, right?" Mom said. "We're just a few houses down. I'll come right over."

"That won't happen," I told her. "I'm not scared of *The. House.* anymore. And I'm a teenager now, you know. I can handle it."

Mom raised her eyebrows. "I'll talk to the Wolfs again, and then I'll let you know my decision."

After dinner, I went to my room and called Beth. "Guess who I might babysit for?" I said when she picked up.

"*Hmm*," she said. "The Muppets?"

"No, silly. I'm babysitting for the family who moved into . . ." I paused for drama, *"The. House."*

"I thought you hated babysitting," she said.

"I don't hate it. I just haven't done it often. But that's not the point. The point is that I'm going to spend the weekend in *The. House."*

"Oh. Right," Beth said.

I was disappointed. I thought she'd be at least a *little* interested.

"Isn't it great?" I went on. "I'll get to explore all its nooks and crannies. And the dad, Bob Wolf—Wolf, isn't that a crazy name? Wonder if they come from werewolves. Anyway, Bob Wolf mentioned *The. House.* has a history—"

"Hope you have fun," Beth broke in. "Speaking of history, I have to go study for the test. Seventh grade is so hard, don't you think? Avery is here right now. We're going to study after we paint each other's nails."

"Okay," I said and waited, hoping maybe, just maybe, she'd invite me over too. But she didn't.

"See you tomorrow," she said and hung up.

I tossed my phone onto my bed. Beth was right. Seventh grade *was* hard. But for me, it was hard for a different reason.

In the end, Mom decided to let me babysit for the Wolfs on the condition that I call her if I needed help. But I knew I wouldn't need any help. I could handle it.

Couldn't I?

Sitter Smarts

Always be aware of
your surroundings.

Chapter 2

That night, when I tried to fall asleep, I kept thinking about Beth and our phone conversation. I couldn't believe Beth wasn't the least bit interested in my babysitting job. *Maybe she was just acting like she wasn't interested,* I thought. *Maybe she was embarrassed because Avery was there.*

The funny thing was, our stories about *The. House.* had made us popular in elementary school. At recess or at lunch, our classmates would crowd around us to listen to our ghost stories. I was usually pretty shy, but whenever we told our stories, I became loud and lively. Beth brought out the confidence in me.

Now, without her, I felt lost. Who was I? Where did I belong? No one gathered around me at lunch anymore. While Beth and Avery sat at a table surrounded by the popular crowd, I sat with a group of quiet kids who barely spoke, even to each other. I hated lunch now. I felt so lonely.

I decided to talk to Beth again. Maybe if we were alone, I'd see the old spark of interest.

The next morning, I stopped by Beth's locker. "My mom decided to let me babysit at *The. House.*," I told her.

She only shrugged and said, "Uh-huh. Good for you." I couldn't tell if she was being serious or sarcastic.

"Yeah," I agreed. "It will be cool to see the inside. And maybe I'll see Lillian!"

"Lillian?" Beth frowned. "Oh, you mean that silly ghost you made up."

"She wasn't silly," I protested. "She was scary. You are the one who added the silly part."

Beth raised her eyebrows. "Whatever."

"What are you doing next weekend?" I asked. "Maybe you could—"

"I don't make plans in advance. I like to keep my options open."

Of course. She didn't want to make plans with me in case something better came along.

A terrifying moment of awkward silence passed. Beth kept glancing past my shoulder, and I searched my mind for something interesting to say. Finally I blurted, "Look! I'm wearing my manga shirt. Better write that down!"

Beth's attention snapped back to me. She stared at me with wide eyes. "What's that mean?"

"Oh, it's just an expression," I shrugged. "You always liked this shirt. Do you want to borrow it sometime?"

"Um, thanks. But no." She wrinkled her nose. "Gotta go!" She brushed past me and disappeared into the swarm of unfamiliar faces.

Ultimate fail. I'd just pushed Beth even further away than she was before.

As I wandered to my first class, I realized what my biggest mistake was. I was only thinking about my own interests. To win Beth back, I needed to show her I was interested in the same things she was—clothes and hair and nails and boys. I needed to *pretend* I was, anyway.

And with my babysitting earnings, I would do just that.

The following Friday, at four o'clock. on the dot, I swung open the gate of *The. House.* and stepped up the sidewalk to the enormous front door. It was chilly out, but I was sweating with nervousness. I'm not sure what I was more nervous about: spending a weekend in a haunted house or spending a weekend in charge of four little kids.

I can handle it, I told myself, lifting my hand to ring the doorbell. But I didn't see a doorbell anywhere, only a large brass knocker with a snarling gargoyle face on it. I lifted it and let it fall with a bang.

Nothing.

I knocked again, and the door fell open. A small woman with large, dark eyes and flowing blond hair stared back at me. She didn't say anything.

"I'm Olivia?" I said. "The babysitter?"

"Ah," she nodded. She swung the door wide, stepped onto the front porch, and leaned into my ear. "I'm sorry," she said softly. "I would love to show you around, but I've already said goodbye to the kids. I don't want to upset them by going back in. My husband will tell you everything you need to know. Go on inside." And with that, she rushed down the sidewalk, leaving me all alone.

I stepped into the large entryway and looked around. Above the door hung a chandelier. As it swung, it creaked and groaned. But the creepiest part of the entryway was six large mirrors, three on each wall. Everywhere I looked, I could see my own worried face staring back at me.

Maybe they are two-way mirrors, I thought. *And on the other side, creatures from the afterlife*

are watching anyone who dares enter the house . . .
I shook my head so hard my curls slapped my face. *Stop it!* I told myself, glaring at my reflection in the mirror.

"Olivia? That you?" Mr. Wolf's voice called.

"Yes," I called back. I stepped from the entry-way into a dark hall with tall ceilings and a curved staircase leading upstairs. At the foot of the steps, yellow caution tape was wrapped around from banister to banister. I couldn't help but shiver. Caution tape means crime. Murder.

Bob Wolf's face appeared at the top of the staircase, startling me. If the stairs were roped off, how did he get up there?

"I'll be down in a minute," he said. He sounded out of breath. "I'm just—well, I'm running late, and I still have to finish packing and can't find my jammies . . ."

"Jammies?" I tried not to giggle.

"Er, pajamas. Yeah, having four kids will make a grown man say things like 'jammies' and 'potty' and 'nappy' and—oh! I need to make sure I remember my . . ." And he ducked away into the shadowy upstairs hall.

I looked around. No toys. No signs of children. No sounds. You would think at least one of the four children would be making some sort of noise, right?

I listened closely. Silence.

Wait, someone was breathing. Someone close.

"*EEEEE!*" something wailed.

I jumped and blurted out a little *ah!* I looked around. The high-pitched scream had come from right in front of me. But no one was there.

"*EEE!*"

Four creatures jumped from behind the staircase. Well, they weren't creatures. They were the Wolf kids. They collapsed onto the floor, giggling.

"Scared ya!" said the boy, Robert.

"You sure did!" I grinned, but inside I was slightly terrified. These kids were going to be a handful.

"Has anyone seen my razor?" Mr. Wolf hollered from upstairs.

"No!" the four children called back.

Little Frannie crawled to me and clutched my leg. "Hi," she said. "Will you play with me?"

"I will," I told her. "But let's wait for your dad. He'll need to give me instructions."

Frannie stuck out her lip. "Don't need 'structions," she said. "Just play!"

"No!" cried one of the twins. "Play with us first!"

"Yes!" agreed the other twin. "Us first!"

"We will all play together. I promise," I said.

A loud crash sounded from upstairs. Then *boom, boom, boom, boom*. Mr. Wolf appeared in the hall, dragging a suitcase and looking frazzled.

"The kids will have to show you around," he said breathlessly. "I'm late!" He shoved a crumpled sheet of paper into my hands. "These are all the phone numbers you'll need. Call or text if you have any problems. In fact, would you mind sending me a text now so I have your number in my phone?"

Nodding, I pulled out my phone and punched in Mr. Wolf's cell phone number from the sheet as he rattled on. "Any problems you can't handle, that is. Of course there will be some problems. These are kids, after all. And, oh! There's food in the fridge and freezer. Bedtime is eight-thirty. Or later, I suppose, if they won't go down. It's the weekend. Sometimes they are allowed to stay up late. Food is in the fridge and freezer—I guess I already told you that. Pizza, mac and cheese, a hamburger casserole that they absolutely love. And make sure they get fruits and veggies every day." He glanced around. "Did I give you the paper with the phone numbers?"

I stared at him, trying to take it all in. Eight-thirty bedtime. Food in fridge. Fruits and veggies every day.

"What about this?" I waved at the yellow caution tape. "What happened?"

"Oh! The banister is a little loose," Mr. Wolf explained. "Don't use these stairs. There are two other stairways in back."

"Got it," I said. "And about the house—you mentioned it has a fascinating history?"

"Yes," Mr. Wolf knelt down, turning his attention to the kids. "Give Daddy a big hug!"

As the kids swarmed over him, he looked up at me. "Murder," he mouthed.

My jaw fell open and my heart nearly plunged out of my chest. "Murder?" I mouthed back.

Outside, a car horn blared. Mr. Wolf straightened. "Oh, it's a fun and exciting story I'll tell you sometime," he said. He launched a jolly wave in my direction and disappeared out the door.

Murder. Here within these walls. Dread crawled up my spine and clutched my shoulders.

Along with my fear, I felt a sense of justification too. I'd been right all along. *The. House.* really *did* have a spooky history. I reached in my pocket for my phone. I had to call Beth!

"Let's play!" Frannie cried, tugging at my leg.

Oh yeah. I'd almost forgotten I had kids to take care of. The phone call to Beth would have to wait.

"I want to meet your brother and sister first," I told Frannie. I smiled at Robert, who was sliding around the wood floor in his socks. "I'm Olivia," I announced. "And you're Robert, right? And you are nine?"

"Yup," Robert answered, barely paying attention to me. He took a running leap and slid all the way down the hall before landing on his bottom. "Are you hurt?" I gasped, but he jumped right up and tried it again.

I turned to the twins. They stood together, watching me carefully. They were completely identical, with two braided pigtails, three freckles on each cheek, and wide blue eyes. They were both wearing jeans and blue sweaters sprinkled with hearts. How would I ever tell them apart? I knew that parents sometimes dressed twins alike to avoid fights over clothes, but couldn't one be wearing the same shirt only in a different color? Or at least different-colored hair ribbons?

"So," I said, smiling at the girls, "are you twins or what?"

"Duh!" yelled Robert from the other end of the hallway.

"And what are your names?"

"Josephine and Jolene," they both responded at the same time.

"Beautiful names," I told them. "Who is Josephine, and who is Jolene?"

"Jolene!" one said, pointing at the other.

At the same time, the other pointed at her and yelled, "Josephine!"

Okay. I was confused. But I knew I'd figure out the difference eventually, so I shrugged it off.

"And you are both seven years old?" I asked.

"Yes," they answered.

"How can you *both* be seven?" I asked with mock curiosity.

"Jo and me were in Mommy's belly at the same time!" one twin explained.

"But Jo was born first," the other twin said.

I looked from one to the other. "Which one of you is Jo?"

"They're *both* Jo!" Robert hollered. "Hey, wanna see my moonwalk?"

"Wow, that's awesome!" I said, watching him dance backward down the hall. I smiled, but inside, my head was exploding. Josephine and Jolene. Identical twins, both nicknamed Jo. I sighed. I was in for a long weekend, that's for sure.

Still, I was absolutely dying to see the rest of the sprawling mansion. I wondered what was in the attic and if there really was a cellar where poor little Lillian had died. I forgot for a second that Lillian wasn't real. I'd made her up.

I'll have to keep reminding myself of that, I thought.

But the murder was real. I shivered, wishing I knew more.

"All right, kids," I said. "I'd like a tour of the house. Who wants to lead the way?"

"Jo will!" one of the twins offered and pushed the other forward.

"We'll need flashlights," Jo advised.

"I'll get them!" Robert offered and whirled away down the hall.

"Why do we need flashlights?" I asked.

"Some of the lights don't work," the other Jo informed me. "Daddy's gonna fix them."

Robert returned with three flashlights. He snapped them on and shined the lights in my face. "I have the power!" he hollered. "I am the all-powerful one!"

"Okay, Mr. Omnipotent. Hand me one of those," I said.

"What's omnipo-whatever?" asked one of the twins.

"It means *all-powerful*," I explained.

"He's not powerful at all," the other twin huffed. "He's just stup—"

"Hey," I stopped her. "Be nice to your brother. Now, let's go. Jo, lead the way."

"Hold my hand," Frannie whispered. I took her hand and followed Jo around the corner into a large living room with tall windows, two couches, a television, and toys scattered across the rug. The room looked normal enough—not even a bit creepy. But something made me shiver. Was this where the murder had happened?

I knelt down and lifted the rug to peer beneath.

"What are you looking for?" Frannie asked.

I was looking for bloodstains, but I couldn't tell her that.

"Sometimes fairies live under rugs," I said. I straightened. "No fairies here! Let's go to the next room."

We toured the rest of the main floor. Nothing seemed too creepy, except a large wood-burning stove in the kitchen. It looked ancient, with heavy cast-iron doors and a snaking pipe leading to a vent in the wall. The thing was gigantic too. A few small children, or a teenager like me, could fit inside. I shivered, thinking of the Hansel and Gretel fairy tale. When I tugged at the doors, they wouldn't budge. I turned away to follow the kids into the next room when I heard a sound. Coming from inside the stove. *Tap-tap-tap. Tap-tap-tap.* Something was inside. And it wanted to get out.

Just a mouse, I told myself. As if mice weren't creepy too. But they were better than dead bodies. Or ghosts.

I tugged the door again. Nothing.

Tap-tap-tap-tap. The taps were coming faster now. *Tap-tap-tap-tap-tap-tap.*

"Olivia!" called one of the Jos. "Come on!"

Little Frannie ran to me and tugged at my hand. She looked wide-eyed at the stove. "Don't let her out," she whispered.

"Who?"

She just shook her head and pulled my hand with surprising strength. "Frannie," I insisted. "Don't let who out?"

"If you let her out, he'll kill her!" Frannie said.

"Who? Frannie, you need to tell me," I said.

Frannie's large eyes spilled over with tears. "I can't!" she wailed.

"Come *on*!" the other Jo called from the doorway.

"Okay," I relented. "Let's go." I knew I wouldn't get any answers from Frannie, at least not while she was sobbing. Maybe later, after she'd calmed down, I'd ask her again.

I followed the kids into a dark, windowless hallway. "Flashlight time!" Robert announced. He flicked on his light and shone it up a set of crooked, narrow stairs. *The lights don't work on the stairwell?* I thought. *Dangerous.*

I couldn't believe Mr. Wolf hadn't mentioned this. I clicked the light switch. Nothing.

"Here we go," I said, swinging my flashlight up and holding Frannie's hand tightly.

The three older kids raced to the top of the stairs, while Frannie and I followed more slowly. At the top of the stairs was a long hallway lined with closed doors. Not a kid in sight. Or a light switch.

I swung my flashlight up and down the hall. "Kids?" I called. "Jolene? Josephine? Robert?"

A door at the end of the hall creaked open. Light spilled into the hallway. One of the twins dashed across the hall and ducked into another room. "Jo!" I said, marching toward the room, Frannie in tow.

"I'm over here!" a voice called from behind me. I whirled around to see the other twin slam a door shut.

Frannie sniffled as if she were about to cry again. I knew it was time to get tough with these kids. I handed the flashlight to Frannie and told her to stand still. Then I stomped down the hall, opening each door and switching on lights. Luckily, all the bedroom lights worked. I found one Jo giggling on the floor of an empty room, and the other Jo peeking out of a closet door in the master bedroom.

"No more funny business," I told them. "You don't want a time-out, do you? I thought you wanted to take me on a nice tour."

The twins nodded. "We're sorry!" they said in unison.

"Now, show me your bedrooms," I said. The twins led me to their room—a normal kids' room with posters, piles of toys, and two small beds. Frannie's bedroom was just across the hall and had bright pink curtains with unicorns floating across.

Everything about the upstairs seemed fairly normal. I realized I hadn't thought about ghosts or murders in at least fifteen minutes.

"Mine next!" Robert yelled, poking his head from around the corner at the end of the hall. I followed him down a second long hallway. I'd never seen a house like it, with two upstairs hallways connecting to make an L shape. At the middle of the other hall was the roped-off staircase, and at the far end was another stairway, with a set of steps leading up and one leading down.

Robert flicked on a light and scampered up the stairs to a landing. "I have my own floor. All to myself!" He pushed open the door, and we piled into his room. After he'd showed me his collection of model spaceships, we headed back to the landing. More stairs led up. "Just a creepy old attic," Robert explained.

We went back down to the second floor, where I tried to get my bearings as the kids scuttled off to their rooms. Three sets of stairs (one roped off), an L-shaped hallway (no electric lights), a room on a landing all its own, another set of stairs leading to an attic (a creepy one, apparently), and . . . ahead of me, a small door I hadn't noticed, with a metal sign on it. I shone my flashlight at the sign and crept closer. The sign read, in stark black letters, "KEEP OUT."

I took a step closer to inspect the sign. It looked old. *Really* old. Like maybe it belonged in Lillian's time. Was this where the murder had taken place?

A swath of cold air suddenly swept down the hall, chilling the skin on my shoulders. Then it was gone, and in its place, a fiery heat.

Yes, said a whispery voice. *Yesss.*

Sweat poured from my forehead, even though inside I felt cold as death.

Was the voice coming from inside my head? Or inside the room?

SSSsss. Not in my head. And definitely inside the room.

I reached for the doorknob and twisted it.

"Stop!" Robert yelled from behind me. I jumped back, my heart a wild animal in my chest.

"Can't you read?" Robert said. "The sign says 'KEEP OUT.'"

I swallowed, hoping my fear wasn't shining on my face. "What's inside?"

Robert shrugged. "Dunno. Don't care."

I was surprised. What nine-year-old boy wouldn't be curious about a KEEP OUT sign?

Unless he was scared of what was in there too.

Sitter
Smarts

Don't tell ghost stories at night.
(Or ever.)

Chapter 3

Frannie came out of her room dragging a doll nearly as big as she was in one hand and a long plastic snake in the other. She dumped them at my feet. I tried not to squirm as the snake slithered across the doll's face, as if it were a *real* snake. "This is my dolly. And her name's Molly. Molly Dolly!"

"Hello, Molly Dolly," I said.

"She has a pet," Frannie went on. "A pet snake. Do you have pets?"

"No," I said. I'd had a cat, Muffy, but she died last year. I didn't want to mention Muffy's death to Frannie in case it brought on tears—either hers or my own.

A chill pricked my skin. A draft must be coming from somewhere, I decided. I glanced up and down the shadowy hallway. Suddenly the upstairs didn't seem so normal to me anymore.

I told each of the kids to bring one toy from their rooms, and we'd all play together in the living room. "And this time, we'll take the lighted stairway. No flashlights needed!"

"But you haven't seen the attic," Robert protested. "It's very spooky. It's where . . ." he trailed off when he saw my face drop. Had he been about to say *where the murder happened?*

We shuffled down the stairs into the living room. I opened the curtains wide to let the last of the day's sun stream through the windows.

"I'm hungry," whined one of the twins.

"Just a sec," I told her, whipping out my phone to shoot off a text to Beth.

> At The. House. Spooky stuff. A murder happened here! You should come over.

> Can't. Busy right now.

One of the twins kicked the other's stuffed bear, sending it skidding across the floor. Jo burst into tears. Meanwhile, Robert was zooming around the room, making airplane sounds. And Frannie was nowhere to be seen.

> I brought some nail polish with me.

I typed quickly. It wasn't true, but I could ask Mom to bring some over.

> You could come over later, and we can do our nails after the kids are in bed.

I shoved the phone back into my pocket and picked up the twin's stuffed bear. Both girls were looking at me with serious expressions. I couldn't tell which had been crying. I made a random choice. "Jo, knock it off. Be nice to your sister."

"I'm *hungry*," she said dramatically and collapsed onto the floor. The other Jo giggled.

"I'll get you some food. But first, we need to clear up this Jo business. I know you both like to be called Jo, but you're twins, and I don't know you that well yet, so I just can't tell you apart. So let's come up with some unique names. Because you're both unique, right?"

"I guess so," one twin mumbled.

"Both unique and both annoying!" Robert shouted, still whizzing around the room.

I chose to ignore him and rummaged in my bag until I found what I was looking for. "Jolene," I said.

One twin looked up. I placed the barrette in her hand. It was one of my favorite barrettes, a round anime eye with sparkles on it. I'd ordered it straight from Japan. Josephine stuck it in her hair. "I'm going to call you Lene from now on. Short for Jolene. Okay?"

I pulled out another barrette, a Supergirl *S*, also glittery. "This one's for you, Josephine," I said. "And I'm going to call you Phine. Short for Josephine."

"Okay!" the twins chirped.

Phine eyed Lene's barrette. I could see a bit of envy in her eyes. "It's okay if you like Lene's better," I told her. "Because you can see it. If it's in your own hair, you can't see it."

Phine shrugged. "I like them both," she said.

"Lene and Phine! Lene and Phine!" Robert shouted. He slid to a stop in front of us. "I like those barrettes! You have good taste."

I blushed a little. I didn't think Beth and Avery would agree. But that was okay.

"I'm going to heat up the casserole, and we'll eat," I said and scurried into the kitchen to find Frannie standing in front of the stove, tugging on the handle.

"She's in there!" Frannie said. "She wants out."

I swallowed. "Nothing's in there," I told her. "Will you help me with the casserole?" I knew that kids her age loved to help out.

But Frannie just shook her head. "She wants out," she repeated.

I took a deep breath and marched to the stove. "Nothing's in here. See?"

I gave the handle a good tug. The door fell open. A dark creature shot out. I screamed and kept screaming, even as the creature sat down on the middle of the floor, licking its paws and eyeing me.

I knelt next to Frannie. "Now, how did a cat get in the oven?"

"Cats make Daddy sneeze," Frannie said. "She's been sleeping under the porch, but it's cold! So I let her in. And when Daddy came downstairs, I put her in the oven so he wouldn't see her. But I want to keep her! Please, can I keep her?"

"I don't know," I said. "But you can't lock animals in ovens or closets or anything like that. They might run out of air. Or get really sick. So don't do that again, okay?"

Frannie nodded. "But I didn't want Daddy to get sick and then throw her away."

I glanced at the cat. She didn't seem feral. She seemed sweet. And I could hear her purring. But still, a shiver crawled up my spine. Black cats were bad luck, right?

Frannie started toward the cat, but I caught her arm. "Don't touch her," I warned. "She needs to be checked by a vet first. And she might belong to someone else."

"So I can't keep her?"

I shook my head. "Probably not, since your dad is allergic." And then I said something without even thinking it over: "But I'll keep her. And you can come visit her anytime you want!"

I couldn't believe I'd just offered to take the cat. A black cat. I shivered again. What had I gotten myself into? I watched as the cat twisted around to clean her tail. The backs of her legs were splotched with white fur. So she wasn't *completely* black. I felt a bit of relief.

The other kids ran into the kitchen, and the cat arched her neck to be petted. "Don't pet her," I told the kids.

"She has to go to the doctor first!" Frannie added.

The twins looked disappointed. "Let's make her a bed," I suggested. "Do you have any old towels or baby blankets?"

The twins ran off to hunt for blankets. We made the cat a bed on the screened-in back porch, where she would be out of reach of the kids but also safe and warm. I called my mom, and she agreed to pick up some cat food. And she reluctantly agreed that I could keep her after the vet checked her out.

After I fed the kids and ate (the casserole really *was* good!), I checked my phone. Still no Beth. Panic swirled around my stomach. Maybe she'd been kidnapped . . . or murdered . . .

I shook my head. *Stop, silly,* I told myself. *She's not dead. She's just ignoring you.*

Somehow that didn't make me feel much better.

The TV in the living room didn't work. Robert informed me the cable guy hadn't come to hook it up yet. "And you don't have a DVD player? Or any movies?" I asked. I'd been hoping for a bit of distraction for the kids, just for a little while. I felt zapped of energy.

"Somewhere in boxes. In the attic," Robert said. "The scary, spooky attic."

I shivered. Robert noticed. "Scaredy-cat!" he said. "Why are you so spooked, anyway?"

The twins, huddled on the opposite couch, stopped chattering and looked at me. Suddenly I knew what to do to fill the time. Something Beth and I loved . . .

"You want to hear a story?" I asked.

At the nods of all the kids, I began: *In an old house on the hill, a house exactly like this one—and I mean exactly, with three different stairways and a hall shaped like an L—lived a beautiful young woman. Her name was Anastasia. Everyone who met her loved her. After her parents died mysteriously, she lived here all alone—I mean, she lived in her house all alone.*

But she wasn't lonely. Anastasia loved to host tea parties at exactly three o'clock every day. And she loved clocks. She had all kinds of antique clocks in the house—tall grandfather clocks, small wall clocks, cuckoo clocks—you name it. She kept all the clocks perfectly timed. When she opened the door at three o'clock to let in her guests, the clocks all chimed at once. But the funny thing was, none of the guests ever saw the clocks. She didn't have one single clock in this room.

Meanwhile, people in town were disappearing left and right! First an old man disappeared, then a young man, then a little girl and a little boy and a young woman.

I paused to catch my breath. Usually at this point in the story, Beth would sing maniacally "Old man, young man, where could you be? Little girl, little boy, D-E-A-D!" And then we would giggle a bit.

But the kids weren't giggling. The twins, holding hands, stared wide-eyed at me. Frannie sucked her thumb. Even Robert was sitting still, waiting.

I leaned closer, happy to have their attention.

It was a dark and stormy night. Well, actually, it was three o'clock in the afternoon, when a young boy . . . Bobby was his name . . . went with his mother to Anastasia's tea party. While the adults chatted over tea, Bobby got super bored. He wanted to explore. No one had ever gone farther than this room, er, I mean, the front room of the house.

When Anastasia wasn't looking, he saw his chance. He slipped out of the room and crept up the stairs. Clocks lined the long hallway. The faces of the clocks were white and ghostly in the shadows. Bobby tiptoed closer. Something was strange about these clocks. Then, with a cry of fright, he realized that the faces of the clocks were human *faces. And the pendulums were made of human bones!*

He ran for the stairs, fast as he could. But he tripped, and knocked his head against a huge grandfather clock. He tried to scramble to his feet. But then the clocks, all at once, chimed one, two, three . . .

A fierce ring interrupted me.

We all screamed.

Sitter Smarts

Don't give out information
to strangers.

Chapter 4

The shrill sound rang again. I let my breath out and gasped for more air.

"It's just the phone," Robert snapped at me. He seemed embarrassed that he'd screamed. He pointed to the telephone.

I leapt up and lifted the receiver. "Hello?"

"Woof!" barked a male voice.

"Woof?" I repeated. Was this some kind of joke? Someone pretending to be a dog to scare me? I swallowed to calm my nerves. "Who is this?"

"Mrs. Woof?" the male voice said.

"Oh, Mrs. Wolf," I said, pronouncing the *L* in Wolf. "I see. No, she isn't here."

"Mr. Woof?"

"No, he isn't here either," I told the caller. "They will be back Sunday. May I take a message?"

My question was met with silence. Then a sharp click. "Hello?" I said to dead air.

"Who was that? Was it Mommy?" asked Phine.

"No, just someone looking for your parents," I said quickly. I wanted to kick myself. Why had I told the caller the Wolfs wouldn't be home until Sunday? Now whoever it was would know I was here alone with the kids. The number-one rule of babysitting was not to tell strangers that the parents weren't home, and I'd broken it.

"Let's play a game!" I suggested cheerfully.

"Yes! Let's play Clue!" Robert said.

I wasn't sure a murder mystery game would be the best.

"Let's play something we all can play," I said. "Clue is too hard for the younger kids."

We settled on Go Fish and spread out on the floor of the living room. Just as I was passing around the cards, the phone blared. I couldn't help but shudder. Was it the strange caller again?

Robert leapt toward the phone, but I put a

hand out to stop him. "Let's let the answering machine get it," I said. I figured if it was Mr. Wolf, he'd leave a message or call my cell.

The answering machine clicked on, but after the beep, all I could hear was heavy breathing, then a click.

Had I made another mistake? Should I have answered the phone and demanded to know who was on the other line?

We played a few rounds of Go Fish. Frannie was too little to understand the game, so I let her be my partner. I found it hard to concentrate, though. "I'm going to get a drink of water," I said and went into the kitchen, staring at the phone as I passed, as though willing it to ring.

I opened the fridge and poured myself a tall glass of water, hoping the cool liquid would calm my nerves. The bright setting sun was peering through the window, drawing a silhouette of me against the wall. I took another drink of water and was about to go back into the living room to join the squealing kids when I froze. A large, hulking shadow enveloped mine. Someone was at the window!

I whirled around and saw a dark figure against the glare of the sun.

I shielded my eyes, my heart in my throat. He could see me, I knew, but I couldn't see him. I dropped to the floor and scooted under a cabinet, chest heaving, tears blurring my eyes. *Could I shimmy out the back door without him seeing me? Maybe I could run home and call for help. But what about the kids? What if he attacked them or kidnapped them? Or worse . . .*

"Kids!" I whisper-shrieked. But they couldn't hear me above their own noises.

I snuck a peek at the window.

The figure was gone.

Then the phone rang.

"Olivia?" the crackly voice on the other end said. It was Mr. Wolf. The knowledge didn't slow my galloping heart much. Whoever was out there was still out there. I scanned the windows.

"Can you hear me?" Mr. Wolf was saying. "I asked how everything is going."

"Oh. Great!" I said, eyeing the kids and the window at the same time. Robert rushed into the room with something in his hands. I couldn't tell what it was. I stepped closer just as he lifted the object—a bucket, I saw now—and turned it over. Legos, hundreds of them—no, thousands, maybe *millions*—spilled onto the floor. Frannie dove into the pile with glee. "Everything here is fine!" I said again. "Did you call earlier?"

"No, we just arrived! Say, could we talk to the kids?"

"Oh, yes, of course!" I said. I handed the phone to Lene, who'd been tugging at my shirt. "Daddy, we got new names!" I heard her exclaim.

I had to be brave. I had to find out what, or rather who, was outside. I tugged on Robert's shoulder. "Come with me," I whispered.

He frowned and shook his head, gesturing to the Legos. "I'm building a starship!"

I knew I shouldn't enlist the help of an innocent nine-year-old, but I was scared. I couldn't investigate alone. "It's a secret mission," I told him. "Come on!"

He sighed and stomped after me into the kitchen. I shivered as I looked at the window. The sun, which just moments ago had been a bright, blinding orb, was now just a dim light tucked behind the trees. "Stand right there," I ordered Robert.

"Why? This is the dumbest mission ever."

"Pretend I'm in real danger. And you're my guard," I said.

I tiptoed closer to the window and looked out. Nothing. Then a noise made my breath catch.

Thud. Thud thud.

The sound was coming from the other side of the house. I turned to Robert, who was staring back at me with wide eyes. "Did you hear that?" I whispered.

He nodded. At the scared look on his face,

guilt filled me. I grinned at him—a shaky grin, but a grin nonetheless. "It's just the wind," I said as breezily as I could. "I hear that sound all the time at my house."

Thud. Thud thud.

The sound seemed closer now.

"I'm sure your parents want to talk to you," I said loudly, ushering Robert into the living room. "Don't tell about the secret mission," I murmured.

Robert snatched the phone from Phine. "Mom? When are you guys coming home?" His voice trembled.

Uh-oh. I'd made a big mistake.

I knelt next to the twins and scooped a few Legos into my hands, watching Robert from the corner of my eye. He scowled into the phone, but then his expression relaxed. By the time he hung up, he seemed to have forgotten about the mysterious thud.

I wish I had.

Sitter Smarts

Don't chat with your friends
on the phone.

Chapter 5

"I'm going to make a phone call," I told the kids. The twins and Robert seemed happily occupied on the living room floor with the Legos, and Frannie was settled with a coloring book and crayons. I went into the front entryway (the mirror-filled horror hallway) where the kids couldn't hear me and dialed Beth's number.

Miraculously, she answered.

"How's *The. House.*?" she asked. "Spooky?"

"Yes!" I breathed. I told her what Mr. Wolf had said about the murder.

"*Hmm,*" she said. "But he didn't give you any details? Are you certain the murder happened in the house?"

"No . . . but why else would he mention it?"

"I don't know. Have you seen that cute guy, Devin Adams?"

"Here? In the house?" I asked, confusedly. Then I blinked. "Was he outside? Was he the one who—"

"Not in *The. House.*," Beth broke in. "I just mean in general. Do you think he's cute?"

"I have no idea who he is. But Beth, there's more. There's been someone lurking around outside. I don't know what to do!"

I heard silence on the other line. Then Beth sighed deeply. "Why are you calling me? You should call your mom or something."

She was right. I *should* be calling my parents. But now that Beth was actually talking to me, I didn't want to let her go. "So, um, about Devin! Are you gonna ask him out?" I asked quickly, hoping Beth wasn't already done with the conversation.

And she wasn't. As she rattled on about the amazing qualities of Devin What's-His-Name, my mind spun. I peered out the door and scanned the front yard. The streetlights had come on, and the twilight cast a gloomy glow over the street. Anyone could be lurking around. And it was almost full dark. I held out my phone and glanced at the time. In another hour, my mom would be here. Could I hold off until then? Or should I call her now? I didn't want to be a baby. I wanted to handle this myself, the way Mitsuko, my manga heroine, would.

"You'll have to point out Devin to me," I told Beth. "Maybe Monday at lunch?"

"Well, now I'm talking about Scott Nesmith," Beth informed me irritably. "Weren't you listening? I can't decide who to ask to the dance."

"Maybe you should hint to both of them," I said. "And see who seems more interested." I honestly had no clue what I was talking about, but I thought I'd read similar advice in a teen magazine.

"That's exactly what Avery said! But I don't want to lead them on," Beth said, then launched into another story about Devin/Scott (I couldn't keep up with which one), and I stopped listening again.

Thud. Thud thud.

The sound was loud. And *inside* the house this time.

My heart chilled. "Look, I have to go," I said into the phone. "I'll call you right back. And if I don't, call 9-1-1!"

"What*ever*," said Beth.

I clicked off the phone and turned to face the possible danger that awaited me. I imagined what the spread of the comic might look like if this was in one of my manga books: a large, creepy house silhouetted against a darkening sky, a lighted entryway with a girl (me), phone in hand, eyes wide, surrounded by my reflection in the hanging mirrors. Endless mes, but only one about to go inside. What else would the illustration show? A face peering out from the attic? A man's shadow in the upstairs window? Is he holding a knife? I wished I could see what the manga reader would see.

I took a breath and stepped into the house. I was met with silence. When I poked my head into the living room, the kids were gone. Legos were scattered everywhere, and a chair had tipped over, as though the kids had left in a hurry. Or been kidnapped.

I couldn't breathe. Fear grasped me tightly and shook me. Why did I leave them alone for so long? What was I thinking?

Thud. Thud thud. Right above my head. Someone was still here. Someone was inside the house.

I grabbed a flashlight from the table and went around to the back stairs, pausing to listen. Silence. I gripped the flashlight in one hand. It was heavy and could serve as a weapon. All I'd have to do is swing at the kidnapper's temple to knock him out. *You've got this,* a voice inside my head told me.

I marched up the stairs and surveyed the long hall. "Robert! Twins? Frannie? Are you up here?" I called. Not a sound.

I took a step. The floorboards underneath me creaked. "Kids?" I called again.

Only the echo of my own voice answered me.

I took another step, and another, until I reached the corner of the L-shaped hall. The other hall was dark and shadowy. I felt around for the light switch, but the wall was smooth. I clicked the flashlight on and shone it down the hall. "Hello?" my voice cracked into a whisper.

Behind me, the floorboards groaned. I whirled just in time to see a furry creature rise from the shadows. I gasped, and the creature lunged toward me, snarling.

The flashlight clattered to the floor and skittered away. So much for a weapon.

I turned to run down the other hall, but another furry creature blocked my way. "*Grrr!*" it said in a squeaky voice. Then giggled.

"*Roar!*" the other creature, the bigger one, lumbered toward me. "*Roar!*"

I picked up the flashlight and poked at the creature's chest. "Robert. Take off the costume now!"

"Did we scare you?" Robert's voice was muffled by the mask over his face.

"We're bears!" said the little creature. Frannie. "It's for Halloween!"

I sighed. "Take off the costumes and put them back where you found them," I ordered. I glanced at Robert. His costume was actually scary, with shaggy fur and a creepy face. And Frannie's was just, well, cute. I couldn't help but smile.

But somewhere inside, I was still frightened. One mystery had been solved. But it still didn't explain the figure looking in the window and the thudding against the house. He could still be out there, lurking. "Where are your sisters?" I asked.

Robert's massive furry shoulders shrugged. "Dunno," he mumbled. "*Roar!*"

"Please stop trying to scare me," I told him. "It's not working. I don't scare easily." My face reddened with the lie. But I realized that, so far, everything that had frightened me ended up having a logical explanation—the noise in the oven (cat), the thudding upstairs (the kids in their bear costumes). Surely the strange person outside had one too.

"Where are the twins?" I asked. "Did they find costumes too?"

Robert shrugged. "No clue."

I helped Frannie take off her bear costume (even though she begged to leave it on—I told her she had to keep it new and clean for Halloween), then headed toward the twins' room.

They weren't there.

I tried not to panic, but scenarios crisscrossed through my mind. What if, while I'd been distracted by Robert and Frannie, the stranger outside had come in and snatched the twins? Or what if they'd fallen into the cellar (like my ghostly Lillian) and couldn't get out?

As it turned out, my panic was justified. But for entirely different reasons.

When I finally found the twins, they were in their parents' bedroom. And they were wearing costumes. *Scary* costumes (although not in the literal sense of the word). They had their mother's dresses draped over them, their faces smeared with makeup. One skirt had a rip in it (I hoped the rip had been there before Phine put it on, but I doubted it), and the other dress had a huge, bright-red lipstick smudge across one sleeve. I stared at them in horror as they grinned back at me.

"You're so pretty!" squealed Frannie, beaming at them.

"This is Mommy's favorite dress!" announced Lene. Of course, it was the one with the rip in it.

I swallowed the lump of dread that had climbed into my throat. As if the twins' costumes weren't bad enough, the master bedroom was a disaster. Clothes and jewelry were strewn everywhere, and a makeup case was spilled open on the floor. I blinked hard, hoping the mess would go away. It didn't.

"Your mom's going to be mad!" I told the twins, although I had no clue how Mrs. Wolf would react. She'd barely spoken two sentences to me. "Take the dresses off immediately, and give them to me. Then you'll need to help me put everything back in its proper place."

"Pooper place! Pooper place!" howled Robert, with a giggle and a dance. He quieted when I glared at him. "Uh-oh, she's *mad*," he muttered under his breath and danced away down the hall.

Frannie tugged on my arm. "Can I help?" she asked.

I smiled at her. "Of course you can. And Robert will help too. Robert!" I called.

Robert reluctantly agreed. I gave him the job of hanging up the dresses we handed to him. ("Because you're so tall," I told him.) I told Lene to put away the jewelry, and Phine and Frannie were tasked with gathering the clothes. I took on the messy duty of cleaning up the spilled makeup.

All the while, I scolded myself for talking to Beth so long on the phone and getting distracted.

Then I realized I hadn't called Beth back. And she, obviously, hadn't called 9-1-1 like I'd told her to. She'd forgotten all about me.

Sitter Smarts

Don't listen to headphones
or loud music.

Chapter 6

After we'd cleaned up the master bedroom, I helped the kids get ready for bed. The kids were tired and didn't argue. My mom texted to see if I needed back up, but I said no. I watched as each of them brushed their teeth and put on pajamas. I settled Frannie into bed first and read her a bedtime story (nothing scary). I did the same with the twins, but Robert declared he was too old for stories. "You're never too old for stories!" I told him, but he shrugged it off.

Now, with the kids asleep, the house was silent. I tiptoed down the hall and passed the KEEP OUT room. I paused to listen. Nothing. Maybe the noises were all in my imagination.

Then I heard the sounds again. *Rustle, rustle.*

Just a mouse, I decided. I didn't like mice, but they were sure better than a ghost or an intruder.

Just as I turned to head down the stairs, I heard a sound that couldn't possibly be a mouse. Something scraped across the floor, as though a heavy object (or a body!) was being dragged.

"Who's there?" I said in a hoarse whisper.

The noise stopped. Whoever, or whatever, was in there had heard me.

"Hello?" I called softly. A bit of rustling answered me. Okay, so if it was a person in there, he (or she) wouldn't make a peep until I left. But an animal might.

Maybe it was a raccoon? Raccoons were clever creatures—they could open drawers and boxes, and they were strong enough to pull an object across the floor. And *The. House.* had been unlived-in for so long that a raccoon (or a family of them) might have taken up residence within its walls.

Still I wasn't about to face a raccoon, flashlight or not. What if it had rabies? What if it took off down the hall, jumped into the kids' beds, and bit them?

I'll investigate in the morning, I told myself. *Or when Mom gets here.*

As if on cue, my phone buzzed. It was Mom.

> Everything OK there? Had to stop at studio. Be there a little after 10. Call Dad if you need anything.

It was only 8:30. More than an hour and a half all by myself until Mom showed up.

> Everything's OK. Kids r asleep. Possible rabid raccoon.

> What?!?

> It's fine. Tell u later.

Downstairs, I switched on all the lights (every light that worked) and settled on the couch. I stared at the blank TV screen, wishing it worked. I was exhausted but my mind was racing. I pulled some comics from my bag and tried to read. But I couldn't focus. I just stared at the panels.

Thud thud. Thud.

I jumped, even though I realized it was just the wind rattling a loose window. Outside, the trees danced, and drops of rain splashed the windowpane. A storm was on its way.

Thud thud. Thud.

I sighed, plugged my earbuds into my phone, and scrolled to the new album by Kudzu, my favorite all-girl band from Japan. I turned it up a notch and closed my eyes.

Someone was shaking me, hot breath in my face. My eyes flew open. Robert stood over me, glaring. "What's wrong?" I cried, whipping off my headphones.

"It's Frannie," he said. "She's been crying for an hour! Didn't you hear her?"

I grabbed my phone and switched off the music. "I fell asleep," I told him, looking at the clock. It was eight-fifty. "She couldn't have been crying for an hour. I've only been asleep for a few minutes!" I said hotly, but inside I felt horrible.

"Well, it *seemed* like an hour," Robert said.

I stood up and ran up the stairs to Frannie's room. Her nightlight lit up her room in an eerie glow. She moaned and sniffled. I sat down at the edge of her bed. "What's the matter?" I asked.

"A slimy sea monster tried to drown me," she sobbed. "He was big and scaly and awful!"

I stroked her hair. "It was just a dream," I comforted. "There's no such thing as monsters."

I regretted telling the scary story. Was that why Frannie'd had a nightmare?

"He tried to drown me," Frannie sobbed again. "And I got all wet."

I felt the sheet. Sure enough, it was damp. Frannie had wet the bed.

I gave her a little hug. "It's okay," I said. "It wasn't a monster. I'll get you some dry sheets and new jammies, okay?"

She nodded as I helped her out of her wet pajama bottoms and into a new pair. I ripped the sheets off the bed and went out into the hall to look for new sheets. Robert stood there, frowning sleepily. "The sea monster again?" he said.

"Again? She's had the dream before?" So it wasn't *all* my fault, at least.

He nodded. "She has it every time she wets the bed. It's been awhile though," he added accusingly.

"Where do your parents keep the bedding?"

He pointed to the closet across from the bathroom.

"And the washer and dryer?"

"Basement," he mumbled.

"Okay. You can go back to bed now. Thanks for your help. You're a good boy."

He raised his eyebrows. "Whatever," he mumbled. I couldn't tell if he was annoyed with me or embarrassed, or maybe a little of both.

I remade Frannie's bed and tucked her in. I propped Molly Dolly and her pet snake at the end of the bed. "Molly Dolly will keep you safe," I told Frannie. "She'll keep the sea monsters away."

She looked at me skeptically. "How?"

"They're scared of her pet snake," I explained. "She waves it in their faces and they go running away, frightened."

Frannie giggled. "A big sea monster is scared of a little snake?"

"Yep," I said. I wiggled the snake in her face. "I don't know how they could be scared of this cute little guy. But they are. Terrified!"

Frannie giggled again and closed her eyes. I bundled up the wet sheets and went in search of the basement.

To tell the truth, I hoped I couldn't find the door to the basement. I didn't want to go down there. Maybe the door would be locked. Or maybe I could wait until morning, although I knew the soiled sheets should be washed right away. Or maybe I could wait until my mom got here, and she could do it. But I didn't want my mom to think I couldn't handle this babysitting job. I had to take care of the sheets myself.

I found the door to the basement near the back stairs. When I opened it, a rush of cold air hit me. I flipped on the light switch. A single bulb danced at the bottom of steep steps. In my head I drew a panel from this page of my comic. A lonely lightbulb casting a dim glow, but in the corners are shadows. Even my imaginary comic book couldn't tell me what I'd find down there.

I hoisted the bundle of sheets and stepped down the stairs. Each wooden rung creaked under my weight.

The basement was huge and open. At once, I was both glad and sorry there were no doors or hallways. If something was down here, I could see what was coming, but I also wouldn't have a place to hide.

Luckily, I didn't have to search far for the washer and dryer; they were just to the right of the stairs. I dumped the load in and twisted the knob. The washer whooshed to life with a familiar, modern sound. I leapt the stairs two at a time and slammed the door shut behind me. That wasn't so bad, I thought. I even felt a bit powerful. I really could handle this job.

By the time my mom arrived, I was settled on the couch with my comics (no headphones this time) and the sheets were tumbling in the dryer. "This is an interesting place!" Mom said, looking around. "And all those mirrors in the entryway! Kind of spooky, if you ask me."

The mirrors are the least spooky thing here, I thought. But I just said, "Mm-hmm."

"How has everything been?"

I thought about everything that had happened. I wouldn't even know where to begin. If it were Beth asking, I'd launch into a detailed story about my trials of the day. But this was my mom. She'd probably grow overly concerned and try to take over the rest of the babysitting shift. So I just said, "Fine. Everything's been fine."

Sitter Smarts

Plan activities to keep the kids
from getting bored.

Chapter 7

The morning was sunny and warm. The kids were all awake by seven, far too early for my taste. With the sunlight streaming through the windows, *The. House.* seemed, if not exactly cheery, at least less scary. My mom had left for her early-morning yoga class, taking the black cat with her. I realized I'd forgotten to tell her about the raccoon (or whatever it was) in the KEEP OUT room. I made a mental note to tell Mr. Wolf about it. I fed the kids toast and juice for breakfast. After they were done eating, the kids stared at me in silence.

"So, um, what do you want to do today?" I asked.

"I want to wear a dress today!" Frannie said.

"Skateboard!" cried Phine.

"Your skateboards are still packed away," growled Robert. He wiped his eyes. He must not be a morning person either.

"I'm gonna wear a dress!" hollered Frannie, grinning. She seemed to have no memory of the scary sea monster dream. "I'm gonna wear a dress all day."

"I'm going to my room," muttered Robert.

"Maybe we should play a game?" I suggested.

"I'm tired of Go Fish," said Lene. "We played it all night."

We'd only played for about fifteen minutes, but I didn't correct her.

"Okay, how about a different game?" I asked.

"Like what? Everything's packed away," Robert said.

"Well, maybe we could make up a game?" I said.

"Jo will make the rules!" Phine said.

"No, *Jo* will," Lene said.

I sighed. I thought we'd gotten away from the Jo nickname.

"I know a game we can play," Robert said, brightening. He caught the twins' eye, and they all grinned at each other.

"Oooh, the *game*!" Phine exclaimed.

"I'm gonna go put my dress on," announced Frannie.

"Wait, what is this game?" I asked. "I need to approve it first."

Robert and the twins eyed each other again. "It's boring for adults," Lene informed me. "You can't play. But you wouldn't want to anyway."

"First I'm going to check on Frannie," I said. Frannie had disappeared upstairs, probably to put on her dress.

Frannie stepped into the hallway wearing a white lacy dress. Backward.

"I'm not sure you should wear that," I told her. "What if it gets dirty?"

Her cheeks reddened. I could tell she really,

really wanted to wear the dress, for whatever reason. "Okay, but just for a few minutes," I told her. I helped her straighten it so it was on correctly.

As we walked toward the stairs, I caught her reflection in the window. She looked like an apparition in her white dress—a ghostly being from the past. Exactly how I'd imagined the ghost of Lillian.

I shivered. *She's just Frannie*, I told myself. *Not a ghost.*

Robert and the twins were huddled at the foot of the stairs, whispering. "We gotta go up to the attic," Robert informed me. "The *haunted* attic."

"It's not haunted," I said.

"That's what I keep telling the ghosts. But they won't listen to me!" Robert giggled. "Wait five minutes, and then you and Frannie come up."

"Okay," I agreed, with hesitation. After they had disappeared up the attic stairs, I turned to Frannie. "Do you know this game?"

She nodded solemnly. "Daddy likes it, but Mommy doesn't."

I wasn't sure if I should be relieved, but if Mr. Wolf was okay with the game, then it couldn't be too bad, right?

We climbed the steep stairs and pushed open the door into the attic. The room had finished walls and a sloped ceiling. Sunlight floated through a small, round window, but otherwise the room was shadowy. Cobwebs clung to the rafters of the ceiling. I immediately covered my head with my hoodie. I hated spiders. "Where are the twins?" I asked Robert, glancing around the attic for them.

"That's part of the game," he said. "Frannie, begin!"

"Aaaooo! Aaaooo!" Frannie sang.

Aaaooo! Aaaooo! the walls echoed. I looked around. It sounded like the twins, but where were they?

Aaaoo! Aaaoo!

"Ready? March!" Robert commanded. He and Frannie fell into step, marching along the edge of the room, next to the wall.

"Come on," Frannie whined, tossing her head at me. "You have to march behind us."

"What's the point of this game?" I asked. "And where are the twins?"

As if in answer, I heard rustling. And a giggle. From *inside* the wall.

I walked slowly behind Frannie. A shiver crept down my back. I didn't like this attic. And I didn't like not knowing where the twins were. "Five minutes," I said. "And then we're going back down—*AAAHHH!*"

I screamed as something grabbed my ankle. I looked down to see Lene, her head poking through the wall, her fingers clutched around my ankle. *How did she get inside the wall?* She grinned up at my shocked expression, then she shimmied backward out of sight. A trapdoor slammed shut. The wall looked smooth as ever.

Robert howled with laughter. "You should've seen your face!" he hollered.

I knelt down and tried to pry the trapdoor open. It wouldn't budge. This house was getting creepier and creepier by the minute. I knocked on the wall. "Twins! Come out of there!"

"I caught you. You're *out*!" was the muffled response from the wall.

Robert swallowed his laughter. "If the twins grab you, you're out. But if you see them pop out first, you bop them on the head. And then *they're* out." He waved his hand around the attic room. "There are trapdoors all over."

I peered at the walls. Sure enough, I could see the faint outlines of tiny doors along the walls. I never would've spotted them if I hadn't known they were there.

"First of all," I told him, "no one is bopping anyone on the head."

"Mommy doesn't like that part either," Frannie informed me.

Robert kept talking as if he hadn't heard me. "We take turns inside the wall. But I don't know about you. You're too big to fit in there."

I knocked on the door again. "Lene? Open up!"

She cracked the door enough so I could wrench it open. She slid out at my warning look. "Game over?" she asked.

"Game over," I said.

I poked my head through the door, blinking to adjust my eyes to the darkness. The space behind the wall was narrow, just wide enough for a small person to squeeze through sideways. "And this passageway goes all the way around the attic?"

"Yup," Robert answered.

What could the hidden space be for? I wondered. *Stolen goods? Smuggling? To hide dead bodies? Or maybe* The. House. *was once part of the Underground Railroad, and escaped slaves hid in here?* I shuddered to think of anyone having to hide out in the passageway for minutes, let alone days or weeks.

I sensed a movement at the end of the passage. "Phine? Is that you?"

"Maybe," she whispered loudly. Her whisper echoed down the corridor.

Can whispers echo? I wondered. I didn't think so. I shivered and shuffled backward out of the passageway. My cheeks felt numb and cold. If any place in *The. House.* was haunted, the attic was definitely it.

A small hand clamped down on my head. "Bop!" said Frannie. "You're out!"

"Watch this!" shrieked Phine, who'd emerged from the secret corridor. She did a series of cartwheels in the room's open space. Lene copied her, and then Frannie tried her own version of a cartwheel.

"I thought we were playing a game," Robert muttered. "This is *boring.*"

"My cartwheels are better than yours!" Lene said to Phine.

"Are not!" Phine defended.

"Let's play tag," Robert said. "Since *she* won't let us play our game." He rolled his head in my direction.

Frannie slapped him lightly with her palm. "You're it!" she screeched.

I sighed. *Oh boy.* I had to figure out something else to keep them occupied. I grabbed my phone and texted Beth.

> I don't know what to do with the kids.

> You probably should've planned some activities.

> Any ideas? Want to come over?

> Maybe later.

"Maybe" was better than "no," but still, later seemed a long time away.

I put a pizza in the microwave. The oven still freaked me out a little, and since the cat had been in there, I didn't think it was exactly clean.

Thunderous sounds and squeals came from upstairs. Lunch wouldn't take that much time. I had to figure out something to do before they broke something. Or got hurt. But what?

Thud. Thud thud.

The sound again. This time, it came from the back of the house. *It has to be a loose window or something,* I thought. I felt braver now in the noon sunlight than I had last night. I was just leaving the kitchen to investigate when the phone rang.

"Hello?" my voice echoed into the receiver.

Nothing. Just a rustling and then silence.

Then I heard it. *Thud. thud thud.* The sound came from the back of the house *and* from the phone. Whoever it was was outside. Right now.

The microwave chimed, and I nearly jumped out of my skin. "Who's there?" I demanded into the phone.

No answer.

I slammed the phone down. "Kids!" I screamed up the stairwell. "We have to get out of here. Now!"

"Olivia?" a deep voice said behind me.

I whirled to see a head poking through the window. I screamed. The head screamed too.

But as I was screaming, I realized I was looking into the most gorgeous brown eyes I'd ever seen.

"I'm sorry I scared you," the guy said. He was leaning into the window, clutching the sill.

"Who are you?" I stammered. "What do you want?" My heart hammered. Killer or not, this guy was cute.

"I tried calling . . ." he said. "I'm Parker Colton." He paused and glanced toward the kitchen. "It smells good in here! Are you making pizza?"

"Um, yeah. But how do you know my name? And what do you want?"

"Mr. Wolf hired me to clean up the yard and fix some of the loose boards on the back of the house. I totally forgot he said there'd be a baby-sitter this weekend. And I'm betting that's you. Olivia, right?"

I nodded. I still felt a little suspicious, despite his good looks. I made a mental note to check with Mr. Wolf to confirm Parker's story.

"You called here?" I asked.

"Yeah. Just now. My dad called last night. He didn't tell you what was going on?"

I shook my head.

Parker grinned. "Dad's not too good on the phone. I'm assuming he hung up on you?"

I nodded. What if this was all a trick? Cute guy distracts babysitter while evil man steals the kids. It didn't seem so far-fetched.

The kids clambered down the stairs, stomping and giggling the whole way. "Pizza!" Robert yelled. When he saw Parker, he skidded to a stop. "Hey, Parker!" he said. "Want some pizza?"

I felt a bit relieved but not completely convinced. Cute boy wins the kids' trust, distracts babysitter; evil man steals kids. Definitely possible.

"I'd invite you in, but I don't know you," I told Parker.

"You can feed me slices through the window," Parker suggested.

I blushed redder than the pepperoni on the pizza.

"I'll get to work," Parker said and climbed down the ladder. I cut up the pizza and fed the kids, hearing Parker's ladder thudding every once in a while against the house. *Thud. Thud thud.* I wasn't afraid anymore, just embarrassed.

I texted Mr. Wolf.

Parker Colton is here. You hired him, right?

Mr. Wolf wrote back.

Oh, I forgot to tell you!

Yes, I hired him. Sorry about that.

When the kids finished eating, I put the remaining slices on a paper plate and went outside. Parker was hammering boards around a back window. He jumped off his ladder as soon as he saw me. "Pizza delivery," I said, holding out the plate to him.

"You're the cutest pizza girl in town," he said.

He was totally flirting with me! My face grew so hot, even my ears felt sweaty.

"I think I've seen you around school. You're a seventh grader?"

I nodded.

"Seventh grade is kinda hard. Everything's so new," he said. "My little sister's going through it right now too. Lucky for her, she has an amazing eighth-grade brother who can show her the ropes." He grinned. "So how's the babysitting going?"

I sat down next to him on the step. "Okay," I said. Soon I found myself telling him everything that had happened—the cat, my bone-clock horror story, Frannie wetting the bed, the chaos the kids had been causing all morning. I poked my head inside every now and then to make sure the kids were okay.

When I told him about Beth's last text, he nodded. "She's right. The kids are bored. You should do some activities. Take them outside."

"I'm not very outdoorsy," I admitted.

"What do you like to do, then?"

I shrugged. "I don't know." I felt embarrassed again. "I like manga."

He raised his eyebrows. "Manga, huh? My sister likes comics too."

Great. So now he was comparing me to his (probably dorky) little sister.

A shriek sounded from inside the house. I looked at Parker. "Yep," he said. "They're definitely bored. Maybe we should take them to the park."

"We?" I said, blushing.

"I'm almost done here," Parker said, waving at the side of the house. "And I can call my sister too. She loves kids."

"Sounds like a great idea," I agreed.

Sitter
Smarts

Take the kids outside to curb boredom
and run off energy.

Chapter 9

I went inside and gathered the kids, who whooped with delight when I told them we were going to the park. I helped Frannie change out of her dress and made sure all the kids had jackets and sturdy shoes. Then we went out the front door to the porch, where Parker and Hannah were waiting for us.

Hannah had long brown hair and glasses. I recognized her immediately from school. She was in my English class, and she always sat in the front row, listening quietly to the teacher, even when the other kids were being loud or wild. I'd never tried to talk to her, and I wasn't sure why. I guess I was always so focused on Beth that I hadn't tried to make other friends.

Hannah smiled at me and then introduced herself to the kids. "I'm Jolene. Lene for short," said Jolene.

"And I'm Josephine. Phine for short," Josephine said. "We're twins!"

"They sometimes call each other Jo," I told Hannah. "Just to warn you. At first it was hard to tell them apart."

"But Olivia gave them new nicknames," Robert added. "She's smart!"

I blushed and looked down at Frannie, who was hiding behind my legs. I remembered what Mr. Wolf had told me—that Frannie was shy around strangers. "It might take a while for Frannie to warm up," I murmured to Hannah. "But she'll come around."

We set off for the park, the twins skipping ahead, with Robert and Parker just behind them. Hannah and I walked more slowly, keeping pace with Frannie. The sun was warm, and I couldn't believe how good it felt to get out of *The. House.*

"This is a nice neighborhood," Hannah said. "I don't live too far from here, but I went to a different elementary."

I nodded. "Do you like junior high so far?" I asked awkwardly, not knowing what else to say.

"I'm still getting used to it," Hannah said. "All my friends are in different classes."

"Mine are too," I said. Although I really had only one friend, or maybe ex-friend, Beth.

We continued on in silence. I searched my mind for something to say. "Parker told me you like comics," I said.

Hannah nodded. "I like Marvel. Superhero stuff. Although I wish there were more female superheroes. Parker said you read manga?"

"Yeah. Manga has lots of female characters. My favorite is Mitsuko from Shadow City."

"I've always wanted to try reading manga, but I just don't know where to begin," Hannah said.

"Start with Legend of the Sleeping Star," I suggested. "That's my second favorite."

I told her a little bit about the premise of the series. I couldn't help getting excited when I talked about manga. My words got faster, and I started drawing with my hands. Hannah listened with real curiosity, unlike Beth, who lately only pretended to be interested. "You can borrow them if you want," I finished.

"Awesome!" Hannah smiled.

"Can I borrow them too?" Frannie asked, tugging at my hand. She'd been so quiet, I'd almost forgotten she was there, except for her sweaty hand in mine. "I can read pictures. Do the books have pictures?"

Hannah and I both giggled. "Comics have lots of pictures," I told Frannie.

"Frannie, you can be our underling," Hannah added.

"What's that?" Frannie asked.

"It means we will train you to be just like us," I explained, grinning.

"Cool! I wanna be just like you."

Hannah and I smiled at each other. I felt bad for thinking she was probably dorky before I even met her. And maybe she was a bit dorky, but I was too.

We rounded the corner to the park. Robert and Parker tossed around a football, while Hannah and I took turns pushing the twins on the swings and helping Frannie go down the slide. As we played, Hannah told me she wanted to write her own comic someday, starring a female superhero.

"I want to write my own comic too!" I told her excitedly. I couldn't believe we had so much in common. "A manga-style comic with a female character. Maybe a Japanese-American girl. I love Japan. I hope to save enough money to travel there someday."

"Is that what you're going to do with your babysitting money? Save up for your trip?" Hannah asked.

I hesitated. "Well, no. Actually, I want to buy a designer handbag. And maybe some tall boots."

"Oh," Hannah said.

I felt foolish suddenly, and unsure. Did I really want a designer bag? A trip to Japan sounded so much better. Or even an illustrated book of Japanese legends I'd had my eye on.

"Well, maybe you could do both!" Hannah said brightly. "Spend a little, save a little."

"Yeah," I said. "Maybe I'll skip the boots. Or the handbag. I guess I just want to fit in."

"I know what you mean," Hannah agreed. "But everyone fits in somewhere."

Her words made me pause. She was right. "I've never thought about it that way before."

"Watch me!" Frannie hollered from the top of the slide. She slid down with her hands in the air, and Hannah and I both clapped.

"My turn!" I said. I bounded up the ladder and squeezed down the slide.

We were having so much fun that I almost didn't hear my name called by a familiar voice. "Hey, Olivia!"

I turned to see Beth and Avery standing on the sidewalk. They both wore boots and skirts and lacy tops. Definitely not park attire. "Olivia!" Beth called again.

I glanced at Hannah. "Are those your friends?" she asked. "You can go over and talk to them. I'll watch the girls."

I wiped the sweat from my forehead and walked slowly toward Beth, conscious of my dirty jeans and old, mud-stained shoes.

"How's it going?" Beth asked. "Are those the kids from *The. House.*?"

"And who is that guy?" Avery added, her eyes on Parker.

"That's my friend Parker," I said. I wasn't sure Parker and I were technically friends yet, but it sounded good.

"Isn't he an *eighth-grader*?" Beth asked, her eyes wide. "He's so cute!"

"Yeah. I've known him for a while," I said, even though "a while" was only a few hours.

Avery stared at me with wide eyes. Beth leaned closer and said, "So, um, is he helping you babysit? I could totally come over later and hang out with you."

At Avery's sharp look, Beth added hurriedly, "And Avery too."

I shrugged. "Maybe. That might be fun." I eyed them closely. "But Parker won't be there."

Their faces drooped in disappointment.

"I guess you could join us now," I said, a bit unsure. I'd been having fun with Hannah, and I didn't want to ruin it. I nodded toward the swing set. "Come meet the kids."

Avery glanced at the swing set and the sand-pit that surrounded it. "I just bought these boots. Like today. I'd better stay on the pavement."

Beth looked from Avery to me to the kids. I could tell she was torn. Finally she pointed to a bench nearby. "We could sit here and watch you guys," she said. "Who's that girl? Doesn't she go to our school?"

"That's my friend Hannah. She's Parker's sister," I replied.

"I totally want to meet her!" Avery said. "Call her over."

I sighed inwardly and trudged to the swing set. When I told Hannah that my friends wanted to meet her, she raised her eyebrows. "They want to meet me? Or Parker?" She rolled her eyes. I laughed and turned back to the kids.

Beth and Avery spent the next half hour giggling loudly on the park bench (probably to catch Parker's attention). Parker just waved at them, as he and Robert joined us on the jungle gym.

Finally, Beth approached, stepping carefully across the grass so her skirt didn't drag on the ground. She looked rather longingly at my scuffed shoes and jeans. "I wish I could join you guys," she said, "but Avery has to go. I'll see you in school?"

I nodded. "I'll text you later," I said. I hoped it hadn't seemed like I was ignoring her.

After Beth walked away with Avery, I looked at Parker, who'd scooped Frannie onto his back and was running around the sandpit. Frannie squealed and laughed.

"I suppose I should get the kids home soon," I said to Hannah. "It'll be getting dark in another hour or so."

Hannah nodded. "Do you babysit them often?"

"No, this is my first time. And it might be my last," I said.

She looked at me, surprised. "Why?"

"I don't think I'm a very good babysitter," I admitted. "The kids were bored until Parker came over. I just didn't know what to do with them. And now that it's getting dark, we'll have to go back inside. And they'll be bored again."

"How about introducing them to something *you* like? Like comics. Frannie seemed interested. And I'm sure Robert would be too. He probably even *owns* some comics," Hannah said.

I hadn't even thought of that. My mind spun.

"We could read some comics together," I said excitedly. "And then the kids could draw their own!"

"Oooh, that's a great idea!" Hannah said. "They'll love it!"

We rounded up the kids and headed back toward our neighborhood. I fell into step with Parker, feeling a little nervous. I'd never really been interested in boys (other than a few celebrity crushes), but Parker was cute. And Avery and Beth had confirmed that fact with their flirtatious giggles.

"Thanks for suggesting going to the park," I told Parker. "The kids had a blast."

"No prob," he said.

"And now I won't be scared if I hear noises outside. I'll know it's just you and your ladder," I said. I felt like I was babbling, but I couldn't stop. "Last night really freaked me out, when you were standing in the window. I feel silly now for screeching and running."

Parker slowed his step and stared at me with a puzzled look. "Last night? I wasn't there last night. I was at soccer practice."

"You were?" I felt the old heart-hammering starting again. "Maybe it was your dad?"

Parker shook his head slowly. "No, Dad was at my practice too. He likes to pretend he's the assistant coach."

I gulped. "Well, someone was at the kitchen window, looking in. The sun was glaring behind him, so I couldn't see his face. When I looked up, he was gone." I closed my eyes for a second at the memory. "Maybe it was just my imagination." I tried to laugh, but it came out as a hoarse hiccup.

"If someone is poking around the house, you should call the police," Parker said.

"If it happens again, I will," I told him, willing my voice to be strong. "It was probably my imagi-nation." But I knew it wasn't. I'd definitely seen someone. And I'd heard the thudding against the side of the house.

"Maybe it was some neighborhood guys poking around," Parker said. He lowered his voice. "I've heard rumors around school that the house is haunted."

"I was the one who started those rumors," I told him. "My friend Beth and I, that is. We made up ghost stories about *The. House.* and told them to our friends at lunch."

Parker grinned. "I see. So, it was probably some kids trying to spook you. Nothing to worry about." His smile fell, and he added in a serious tone, "You still should've called someone."

"I know," I said. "But I was trying to be brave, you know? And not be a scaredy-cat."

Just then, ahead of us, Phine crumpled to the ground. I rushed toward her just as Lene shouted, "Get up!"

"I can't!" Phine wailed. "I'm so *tired*!" She placed a hand on her forehead and sighed dramatically. "I'm never going to make it. I'll *die*!"

Hannah grinned at me as I knelt and tried to

lift Phine to her feet. "Good luck," she said. "Looks like you have your hands full!"

"Literally," I mumbled. "Come on, Phine. We're almost home."

I finally got Phine to her feet, and she made a great show of stumbling and sighing loudly down the sidewalk. Frannie giggled and copied her. I sighed too, but mine was for real. Hannah shrugged and said, "If you can't beat 'em, join 'em." Then she, too, started sighing and wiping her brow and lurching forward.

"Girls are so weird," Robert grumbled.

"Hey!" I said, punching him playfully on the shoulder. "I'm a girl. And I'm not weird."

"Sure," Parker nodded. "Whatever you say."

I glared at him, but he had a twinkle in his eye and a teasing smile. He was flirting with me again! I turned a solid shade of red and looked away.

When we got back to *The. House.*, Parker went around back to put his ladder in the shed. He came back to the front porch and whispered to me, "I checked around and didn't see anything suspicious."

"Thanks," I told him.

"I'll see you in English class," Hannah said to me. "And maybe at lunch, too?"

"Sure! And I'll bring you those books," I told her.

The two waved and disappeared down the street.

And then we were alone in *The. House.*

Sitter Smarts

Stay out of forbidden rooms.

Chapter 10

Inside, I switched on all the lights, even though the sun was still shining. I went into the kitchen and pulled the curtains closed. If someone came prowling, at least he wouldn't be able to see in. And maybe, like Parker said, it was just some kid playing pranks. After all, I hadn't seen his face, just his silhouette. As I fixed dinner, I kept my phone within reach just in case, glancing often at the window to catch any shadows.

After we ate, I asked Robert for paper and colored pencils, gathered the kids in the living room, pulled all the shades tight, and took out my manga books. I lay on the floor, elbows propped, with the books spread out in front of me. The kids piled around. I read the most adventurous—and least spooky—book aloud. They listened quietly, every once in a while asking questions about the characters.

Then I handed out paper and pencils and told them to create their own comic story.

"But I can't spell!" Lene cried.

"And I can't even read," Frannie said.

"That's okay. See how the story is mostly told in pictures? You can all draw pictures, right?" I asked.

They nodded and crouched over their papers. Frannie scribbled some circles and then looked up at me, tears brewing in her eyes. "I can't draw," she said.

I leaned over her paper. "Sure you can," I told her. "Just draw eyes and a mouth on the circle to make a face. Like this." I drew eyes and a smile on one of the circles.

Frannie nodded and scribbled eyes, noses, and mouths on the circles. She pointed at two of the heads. "See? They're talking to each other!"

The comic-drawing was a success, except for a few arguments over whose turn it was to use some of the more popular colors. Robert's story was a bit gory (a zombie takeover), but it had a happy ending at least. Frannie's story featured her doll, Molly, and the pet snake. Lene and Phine both wrote about a pair of SuperTwins superheroes. Lene wrote about one twin, and Phine wrote about the other, and at the end, the SuperTwins joined together in the same save-the-world ending. I was amazed at their imagination. "You should show these to Hannah," I told them. "She'd love the girl superheroes."

My phone buzzed. A text from Beth.

"Can I come over?"

I typed back,

"Parker isn't here."

"That's okay. Ten mins?"

I read the text twice to make sure I was reading it right. Why did Beth want to come over?

Parker wasn't here. She clearly didn't have much of an interest in *The. House.* Or in the kids. Or me. *Maybe Avery is busy*, I thought. *Or maybe she wants help with her math homework.*

Even though I couldn't figure out her reason, I felt a prick of hope inside. Beth was coming over. We would be friends again, and that's what I wanted. Right?

At her knock, I swung open the door. She stepped into the entryway, with its walls of mirrors.

"Whoa," she whispered. I met her eyes in our infinite reflections. Trillions of Beths, trillions of me.

"Come on," I said, and tugged her into the house.

She eyed the caution-taped stairway warily. "What happened there?" she said.

"Broken banister," I said. "Mr. Wolf roped it off so the kids wouldn't use it. Where he got the caution tape, I have no idea."

Beth hugged her arms and gazed up at the ceiling and down the hallway. "Remember all the stories we used to make up about this place?"

"Of course I do," I said. "Lillian the cellar-ghost and Anastasia the bone-collector were my favorites."

"I loved Peter the penny-boy," Beth said.

"Ooh, I forgot about that one!" I said, and lowered my voice. "Peter's parents loved money more than him. They lived all alone in a big house—this house—*The. House.*—and they made Peter do all the chores while they lounged around in expensive clothes."

"At night, they locked him in the turret," added Beth. "In his ragged clothes."

"He vowed revenge . . ."

"And stole pennies, one by one, from his parents' stash."

"Sometimes in the middle of the night, he threw pennies out the window to beggars on the street below."

"*Ping! Ping! Ping!*" chimed Beth.

"One night his parents caught him . . ."

Beth popped her eyes open, wrapped her hands around her neck, hung her tongue out, and made gagging noises. It was all I could do not to laugh.

"And they punished him with . . ." I continued.

"Death!" we both whispered.

"Sometimes, you can still hear him in the turret," I murmured, "dropping pennies."

"*Ping! Ping! Ping!*" Beth sang.

We both giggled. It was like the old Beth had never left.

Then Beth rolled her eyes. "Gosh, we were lame," she said.

"I don't think it's lame," I snapped.

"I'm so glad we're older now," Beth said, as if she hadn't heard me. "And done with all those silly stories." Suddenly she paused, and her eyes widened. She gripped my arm. "Do you hear that?" she whispered.

"What?" I whispered back. Had she heard the mysterious thudding? I shivered, listening.

"*Ping! Ping! Ping!*" Beth sang, then collapsed into laughter. "Gotcha!" she said.

I tried to hide my annoyance. "Let's go check on the kids."

The kids barely looked up when I led Beth into the living room. They were intent on their comics. "Read mine!" Lene thrust her pages into my hands.

Beth *oohed* and *aahed* over the kids' comics, but I could tell she was faking interest. She kept glancing at her phone. She was definitely more interested in whoever kept texting her. The old Beth was gone again, replaced by the new—and rude—version of Beth.

"Time for bed!" I told the kids. I turned to Beth. "Want to help me get them to bed?"

"I suppose." She sighed.

The kids were so exhausted from our day at the park that they didn't argue. Frannie was the only one who wanted a bedtime story, and she fell fast asleep two pages in. I met Beth in the hallway, where she stood in the glow of her phone. "This house is so weird," she said. "How can you stand it? It smells like . . . like *old*."

"I like *The. House.*," I said, defensive. And I realized I really did.

We headed toward the back stairway, Beth texting as she walked. Then she stopped in her tracks and gripped my arm. "Do you hear that?" she whispered.

"Ha-ha," I said.

"No, seriously! It's coming from over there." Beth gestured toward the end of the hallway. The KEEP OUT room.

We stood listening to the rustling and creaking that sounded from the other side of the door. "I think it's just a raccoon or squirrel," I told her. "I'll go get a flashlight. Wait here."

Beth shook her head. "I am *not* waiting here. I'm way too freaked out."

We tiptoed down the steps, and I grabbed the flashlight. Then we returned to the KEEP OUT door. Beth stared at it, her face white. "What if this is where they kept Peter the penny-boy? Not in the turret, but *in that room*."

"We made that story up, silly," I said.

Beth shook her head. "We *think* we did, but what if some ghost whispered it to us in the middle of the night? And we woke up with the story in our heads, thinking we invented it, but it's really true?" Her voice shook. After she had teased me by trying to creep me out, I couldn't believe how frightened she suddenly was.

"Well, let's have a look. If it's really Peter in there, we can release him!" I giggled, but Beth didn't move a muscle.

"You open the door," I told Beth, "and I'll stand here with the flashlight, in case something pops out at us."

"I'm. Not. Touching. That. Door." Beth took a step backward, glancing over her shoulder.

"Fine. I'll do it." I grasped the doorknob. It was cold, as though carved from ice. I snatched my hand away. Why was a doorknob, inside the house, so freezing? I remembered what I'd learned about ghosts from TV shows about haunted places. Ghosts were cold. Like death. In one episode, a woman claimed a ghost kissed her cheek and left behind frost-bitten skin in the shape of lips.

"Open it!" hissed Beth behind me.

I wrapped my sleeve around my hand and touched the doorknob, half-hoping it would be locked. The knob swiveled under my grip, and I pulled the door open.

Frigid air slammed my face.

Something crackled and rolled toward us.

Beth yelped and jumped back. "What's in there?" she gasped.

Blood rushed to my ears, roaring so loud I couldn't hear anything. I flicked on the flashlight and shone it into the room's depths. Then I laughed.

"What?" Beth peered over my shoulder, and then she laughed too.

Inside the small room (more like a walk-in closet) stood piles of boxes. Boxes of toys, that is, with rolls of Christmas wrapping paper draped over them. Wind blasted through an open window, rustling the paper. An old rocking chair huddled in one corner. At each gust of wind, the rocking chair moaned and creaked. No one was inside. All the sounds I'd heard were caused by wind.

"Well, I certainly feel stupid," Beth muttered.

"I hereby dub this house The House of Logical Horrors," I said, ducking into the room. "Every creepy thing has been explained." Everything but the silhouette outside the kitchen window, that is. And even that might have an explanation. I just hadn't discovered it yet.

I waded through the boxes and pulled the window shut.

"The Wolfs sure do their Christmas shopping early," Beth said, kneeling down to gaze at the toys. "Look at this doll carriage! I would've killed for one of these when I was a kid."

Before I had a chance to respond, small footsteps sounded down the hall, charging so fast we had no time to shut the door. Frannie barreled into the room and launched herself into the pile of boxes.

"Is that a pony waterfall?" she squealed. She tugged one box from the pile and hugged it to her chest. "A pony waterfall! A pony waterfall!"

"Uh-oh," Beth said. "You're in big trouble now, Ms. Babysitter."

I steered Frannie out of the room before more damage could be done. Somehow I managed to pluck the waterfall from her and toss it to Beth.

"A pony waterfall?" I said. "That's a crazy dream you just had, Frannie."

"Wasn't a dream. I *saw* it!"

"One time, I had a dream about a . . . um . . ." I couldn't think fast enough.

"A rainbow cloud!" Beth interrupted. "Hundreds of hyenas lived on that cloud."

"They danced and laughed like this—"

"*EEE!*" Beth screeched while I kicked up my legs in a sort of Irish jig.

Frannie stared at us and rubbed her eyes. "A rainbow cloud?"

I took her hand and led her down the hall. "You better go back to sleep now," I told her, "so you can dream about your hyena ballroom."

"It was a waterfall," Frannie muttered.

"A hyena waterfall aquarium!" I said.

Frannie shook her head as she climbed into bed. I tucked the blankets around her. "Sweet dreams," I said.

"Think she'll believe that bit about the waterfall being a dream?" Beth asked later, when we were back downstairs.

I shrugged. "I hope so. But I'd better tell the Wolfs, just in case." I sighed. I made a mental note to make a list of everything I needed to tell the

Wolfs when they returned in the morning. It was a long list.

"So, can I ask you something?" Beth said, her voice urgent.

I nodded, wondering what it could be.

She thrust her hands in front of my face. "Do you like my nail polish?"

I blurted out a laugh. "Seriously?" I asked.

Beth's expression fell. She tried to pull her hands away, but I grabbed her fingers. Her nails were painted bright blue with purple swirls. "Very cool!" I said, and I meant it.

She gave a half smile, but I could tell she was still annoyed. "I know you think nails and hair and stuff is silly, but I don't."

"I don't think it's silly," I told her. "It's just not my thing."

She looked down at my fingernails. Her nose crinkled a little. "You should really try painting those sometime. Especially if you want to go to the dance with Parker."

My face turned as hot and red as a desert sunset. I looked away. "I never said I wanted to go with Parker. I forgot all about the school dance," I added, which was true. Of course, now Beth had put the idea in my head.

"Here," she said, whipping out a bottle of polish from her handbag. "Let's try this."

Beth swiped polish on my nails (in between glances at her phone). I admit I did like the polish. It was dark silver with black glitter, the kind Mitsuko might wear. As Beth polished away, I said, "Can I ask *you* something?"

At her nod, I went on. "Why did you come here tonight?"

She frowned. "What do you mean?"

I took a deep breath. "Well, we don't really hang out much anymore. Not even at school. So . . ." I trailed off, feeling tears suddenly filled my eyes. I did *not* want her to see me cry.

"That's why I'm here!" she said. "Now that I'm friends with Avery, I don't have much time to hang out with you. And you don't have any other friends, really."

"So you feel sorry for me," I spat, anger boiling up over my tears.

"Well," she said slowly.

"I know about your fashion notebook," I went on. "*Yuck* next to my name."

She stared at me, eyes wide. "It's all just in fun. Like a joke. We pretend to be Fashion Police. Like judges on those reality shows, you know?"

"It's not funny if you're on the receiving end," I informed her.

She covered her face with her hands. "I'm sorry. I know the notebook is awful. It really is. I'll get rid of it, no matter what Avery says."

"Good," I told her. "Because it's really mean. Not just to me, but to everyone else you write about."

"I never really thought about the notebook being mean," Beth admitted. "I just thought it was fun. And writing down what everyone else is wearing gives me ideas. Like, right now I'm wearing these striped socks and my checkered skirt, because when I saw Maria Ramos mixing patterns, I knew I could too—"

Beth prattled on breathlessly. She reminded me of myself when I talk about manga.

"I suppose I'm boring you," Beth finished.

I shook my head. "It's okay that we have different interests," I told her. "I guess that's what happens in junior high. And just think about high school! What will we be interested in then?"

Beth laughed.

"But . . . just because I don't care about fashion doesn't mean you should totally ignore me."

Beth sighed. "Everything is just so difficult. I mean, I'm friends with Avery. But also with you. And it's so hard to choose!" Her voice trembled like she was about to cry.

I was the one feeling sorry for her now. "You don't have to choose," I said, tugging her hands away from her face. "It's okay to have more than one friend. I have other friends now too. Like Hannah."

Beth blinked away her tears. "And Parker," she said teasingly.

I rolled my eyes and looked down at my hands. "Think this polish will make him ask me to the dance?" I giggled.

"Um, you smudged one!" Beth giggled too.

Footsteps sounded on the front porch. Beth leapt to her feet, but I grabbed her arm, careful not to smudge another nail. "It's just my mom," I said.

I went to the front door and peered out. Sure enough, it was my mom. I let her in, and she took one look at Beth and wrapped her in a hug. "We've missed you at our house!" Mom said.

"Seventh grade has been really busy," Beth explained.

Mom eyed me over Beth's shoulder. I shrugged and nodded.

"Well," Mom said. "Tell me about junior high!"

Sitter
Smarts

Keep a list of things to tell parents
when they get home.

Chapter 11

After Beth left, Mom made herself a bed on the couch and fell fast asleep after doing her yoga-like breathing meditations. I tried them too, but they didn't calm my mind.

Lying awake, I finally pulled out a notebook and made a list for the Wolfs. I wrote down what the kids had eaten for each meal and what time they'd gone to bed. Then I wrote down the various things that had happened that the Wolfs should know about.

1) Cat: Frannie let a cat inside and put her in the woodstove to hide her. I let her out, and we put her on the back porch. My mom took her to the vet. We might keep her if no one claims her. (Frannie is welcome to visit anytime!)

2) Nicknames: I gave the twins new nicknames to help me keep them straight. Jolene: Lene and Josephine: Phine.

3) Horror stories: I made the mistake of telling the kids a scary story about a woman who made bone-clocks. Sorry! Sometimes my imagination works overtime.

4) Phone calls: The phone rang and scared the living daylights out of me. But it was just the Coltons asking about doing work on the house. Mr. Colton didn't leave a message or anything.

5) Dress-up: The kids got into Mrs. Wolf's makeup and clothes. One of the dresses ripped at the bottom. I will pay for any repairs!

6) Bedwetting: Frannie had a scary dream (I hope it wasn't because of my bone-clock story) and wet the bed. I changed and washed the sheets.

7) Comics: I had the kids make comic books. They loved it, and they are very talented (be sure to read the twins' comics. Very creative!)

8) KEEP OUT room: I heard noises in the KEEP OUT room so I decided to investigate. The window was open, so I closed it. Meanwhile, Frannie got out of bed and ran into the room. She saw the pony waterfall. I tried to convince her it was just a dream. Hopefully she'll forget about it.

9) Apology: Sorry for all my mistakes! I loved babysitting your kids. They are great!

I re-read my last entry, realizing I meant every word.

In the morning I woke early, just as the sun was rising. I crept up the stairs and checked on the kids. All were sound asleep. When I went back downstairs, Mom was awake, doing her morning yoga stretches. "I can stay and help you feed the kids when they get up," Mom offered.

"Not necessary," I told her. "I can handle it."

"I know you can," she said with a smile.

Soon the kids clattered down the stairs. "Mommy's coming home today!" chirped Frannie. "And Daddy too!"

"They'll be happy to see you," I said.

I fixed breakfast, and, after the kids ate, they went into the living room to add more to their comics. I cleaned the kitchen, humming to myself. I even opened the kitchen curtains wide to let in the sun.

I thought about everything I'd learned over the weekend. I'd been so nervous about taking care of four kids, but now it all seemed to come naturally. I was no longer spooked by *The. House.* (not really, anyway), and I had now accepted my ending (or changing) friendship with Beth. I could make new friends, just as she had. I'd already made one, and I knew there would be more in my future.

When the Wolfs' car crunched up the driveway, the kids abandoned their comics and raced to the door. Mrs. Wolf almost toppled over with the force of four kids hurtling at her, and Mr. Wolf stood behind her, panting from lugging their suitcases up the porch steps.

"Show you our comics!" Frannie squealed and tugged on Mrs. Wolf's arm. Mrs. Wolf smiled at me and followed the kids into the living room.

"Whew!" Mr. Wolf said, wiping his brow. "How did everything go?"

I handed him the list, watching nervously as he read through it. A smile tugged at the corners of his mouth. "Looks like everything went well!" he said.

"Aside from those problems," I said, pointing at the list.

"Ah, no biggie. Making the list was a great idea! You're a thoughtful babysitter." Mr. Wolf grinned at me.

Wow. I hadn't expected a compliment. "Thanks," I mumbled.

"I'll walk you home," Mr. Wolf offered. "That way, I can thank your mom too."

I went into the living room to say goodbye to the kids. I hugged each of them.

"Will you come play with us again?" Frannie asked.

"I hope so," I told her.

The twins held out the barrettes I'd used to keep them straight. "Keep them," I said.

"You're pretty cool," Robert told me solemnly. "Even for a girl."

"Thanks, buddy," I said. "You were a big help."

As Mr. Wolf and I walked down the street to my house, I told him the kids had shown me their attic game. "Do you know what the secret passageway was used for?" I asked. "Was it part of the Underground Railroad?"

Mr. Wolf nodded. "I think so!" he said. "I've been doing some research. Hiding slaves was illegal, so people didn't keep records, but the dates line up."

Wow. I always knew *The. House.* was special. But I never imagined it was such a part of history. I thought about all the people who may have passed through there. Maybe even my own ancestors.

I had more questions to ask. "So," I began, "The other day, you said there was a murder in the house?"

He turned to me, surprised. "Oh! Gosh, I hope I didn't scare you with that. There was a murder. But it didn't happen in the house."

Would've been nice to know that, I thought, but didn't say it.

"You want to hear the story?" Mr. Wolf said in an excited voice. "Or will it scare you?"

"I'm no scaredy-cat," I told him. It was mostly true.

"So, a hundred and fifty years or so ago, a young woman named Ana . . ." he paused. "Anabelle, maybe?"

"Anastasia?" I whispered.

He shook his head. "No. Or was it Lillian?"

"Lillian?" I gasped.

"No. I've got it! Lily-Anna."

My heart pounded. The coincidence—if it *was* coincidence—was bizarre. Lillian, the cellar-ghost. Anastasia of the bone-clocks. Beth and I had made up those names, hadn't we? But here was Mr. Wolf, telling me a true story about Lily-Anna.

I tuned back into what Mr. Wolf was saying. "Lily-Anna was a lovely young woman who lived in the house with her parents. She had two suitors who wanted to marry her. Their names were Edgar and . . ."

"Not Peter!" I cried, thinking of Peter the penny-boy.

Mr. Wolf frowned in confusion. "No. Edgar and Philippe."

"Okay," I breathed, relieved.

"Anyway, the two of them courted her. At last, she made her decision to marry Edgar. Philippe went wild with jealousy. He sent Lily-Anna letter after letter, begging her to reconsider. He even started prowling around the house, banging on windows and doors to try to get in. One day, Edgar caught him at the kitchen window, staring inside. He told Philippe to leave, but Philippe refused. So Edgar challenged him to a duel. You know what that is, right?"

I nodded. "It's an old custom. Two guys would stand back-to-back, take ten steps, then turn around and shoot at each other at the same time."

Mr. Wolf bobbed his head excitedly. His face was flushed. I couldn't believe an adult like him could be so entranced by a creepy story. Maybe I wasn't so childish after all for liking ghost stories.

"The two men went to a field, five miles from town. Lily-Anna was beside herself with worry. Edgar wasn't the best shot, she knew. But as it turns out, Philippe was the one who was killed."

"So the good guy won," I said. "Is the story true?"

"A lot of it is hearsay," Mr. Wolf admitted. "Although I found an old newspaper clipping that mentioned Philippe's death from a gunshot wound. But there's more! Supposedly, Lily-Anna kept all her letters from Philippe hidden in a secret compartment in the house. No one has ever found them."

"Really?" I breathed. "Wouldn't it be cool to find them?"

"Definitely. I'm going to search every nook and cranny until I do!" Mr. Wolf said. "And there's one more thing." He paused his footsteps and turned to me. "You sure you aren't scared?"

"No."

He lowered his voice. "According to legend, the ghost of Philippe still lurks outside the kitchen window at sunset, trying to get in."

A cold chill grasped my bones. Philippe. At sunset. Lurking around the kitchen window.

Had I seen a ghost?

I closed my eyes and swallowed.

"What's wrong?" Mr. Wolf asked. "I knew I shouldn't have told you. I'm sorry. This story just excites me so much. You don't believe in ghosts, do you?"

I looked at him. "I don't know," I said. "But there's something I need to tell you—something I didn't write on the list."

I explained the figure I'd seen outside the window. "I should've called the police," I said. "But I thought it was my imagination. And maybe it was. Or maybe it was some neighborhood kids poking around. I only saw him for a split second, and then he was gone."

Mr. Wolf nodded. He didn't seem too concerned. "I'll go over the tapes," he said. "I installed security cameras all around the outside of the house. Did I forget to tell you that? I'm so scatterbrained!"

I swallowed, feeling only a bit of relief. "A security camera wouldn't spot a ghost, would it?" I said.

Mr. Wolf laughed loudly. "I don't believe in ghosts," he said a bit too excitedly. "But I like ghost stories. And this is a great one! I hope it doesn't keep you from babysitting again. You're number one on our list!"

"I'll babysit again," I told him firmly. "Ghosts don't scare me anyway." (It was only a half-lie. They did scare me, but also fascinated me.)

At my doorstep, Mr. Wolf paid me in cold, hard cash. The first money I'd ever earned. And, above all, I'd had fun doing it.

That night, I texted Beth.

> I have an awesome story for you. Ghosts! Murder!

> Can't wait to hear! Tomorrow after school?

Then I gathered the first issues of Legend of the Sleeping Star to give to Hannah. I flipped through them, feeling the old excitement I'd always found within their pages. I hoped Hannah would love them as much as I did.

The black cat, which had been checked out by the vet, waltzed into my room and jumped on my bed, purring. I petted her soft fur, hoping no one would claim her. I decided to name her Mitsy (short for Mitsuko).

After I turned out the light, I stood at my bedroom window, looking out at the shadowy street. I couldn't see *The. House.* from my window, but I knew it was there behind the trees, waiting for me to unearth more of its secrets.

About the Author

Jessica Gunderson grew up in the small town of Washburn, North Dakota. She has a bachelor's degree from the University of North Dakota and an MFA in creative writing from Minnesota State University, Mankato. She has written more than fifty books for young readers. Her book *Ropes of Revolution* won the 2008 Moonbeam Award for best graphic novel. She currently lives in Madison, Wisconsin, with her husband and cat.

Want more of the Babysitter Chronicles?
Check out this sneak peek of

Kaitlyn and the Competition

I couldn't help giggling at the giant sunflower—
AKA my older sister, Eve—as she walked into
my bedroom.

"Ha-ha. Real funny, Kaitlyn," my sister said
with a scowl. "These petals around my head
weigh a ton. I need a warm bath, twelve hours of
sleep, and a long vacation."

I stared at the yellow felt petals around Eve's
face and the bright green leotard covering her

arms and legs. "Looking at you sure makes me appreciate babysitting. It's a much better job than working at children's birthday parties," I said.

"Any job is better than working at children's birthday parties. You don't even want to know-how I lost some of my petals. It involved rowdy six-year-olds with very poor scissor etiquette." Eve threw her petal headpiece onto my rug and walked toward my bed.

I blocked her path. "Please don't sit on my new comforter."

"I won't stain it, Kaitlyn," Eve said.

"Last week, you came home with chocolate all over your penguin costume. The week before, you had clumps of dirt in your duck feathers. I just don't want anything tarnishing my new comforter," I said. "No offense."

"Offense taken," Eve said. But fortunately she changed course without saying another word and sat on my old wooden desk chair.

I pointed at a bright pink splotch on her bright green tights. "What is that on the knee of your tights? Bubble gum? Cotton candy? Vomit medicine?"

Eve sighed. "I'm too tired to care. I hate my job."

I didn't blame her. Her job was pretty terrible. She worked as a face-painter at children's parties. She was paid minimum wage and had to wear awful costumes.

"There was one good thing about the party today, besides earning money," Eve said. "The guy who made balloon animals there was *sooo* cute. We snuck off for a few minutes to eat pizza in peace and exchange phone numbers."

I wrinkled my nose. "You snuck off during the middle of the party? To flirt with a guy and eat your client's pizza?"

"Sheesh, Kaitlyn. You make it sound like we ran off with the birthday girl's presents," Eve said.

"It just seems unprofessional. Like Mom says, '*Si vale la pena hacerlo, vale la pena hacerlo bien.*'" That was Spanish for, "If something's worth doing, it's worth doing well."

"Oh, lighten up," Eve said. "You know, you'd be happier if you chilled out a little."I crossed my arms. "I'm not taking advice from a giant, tattered sunflower with pink mystery gunk on her knee."

"Fine. You won't feel so superior tonight when I'm at the hottest party in school and you're in your room reorganizing your closet or whatever."

"I'm going out tonight," I said.

"Where?" Eve asked.

"I'm babysitting."

Eve snorted.

I glared at her. "Save your snorts for the next time you have to wear a pig costume. Babysitting is a lot better than dressing up as a dorky flower and painting the faces of kids who cut off your petals and smear strange stuff on your stem."

"Whatever. See ya." Eve left my room.

I called out, "Wouldn't want to be ya!"

But I sort of did want to be her.

Obviously, I didn't want Eve's horrible job. And even if I had her job, I would never take an unauthorized, unprofessional break to eat pizza and trade phone numbers and flirt with a cute boy.

But I would "want to be ya" if it meant getting invited to the hottest parties at my school. Or even the not-so-hot parties. I wouldn't mind a warm party or even a lukewarm one.

Eve was three years older than me. But it wasn't our age difference that made Eve the life of the party and me . . . well . . . not even at the party. When Eve was thirteen like me, she'd gone to a bunch of bar and bat mitzvah parties, even though we weren't Jewish. At fifteen, she'd been invited to a ton of Quinceañera parties and had a zillion friends at her own Quinceañera party. And this year, she'd spent many nights at Sweet

Sixteen parties. I, by contrast, hadn't been to a party in months.

The difference in our popularity couldn't be blamed on our appearances either. Everyone said we looked alike. We both had wavy brown hair and dark eyes and heart-shaped faces. Simply put, I was a shorter, less-curvy version of my sister.

It was our personalities that made us so different. I'd always been careful. Eve had always been careless. I didn't want to leave the house with a wrinkle in my clothes or a hair out of place. Eve didn't even notice stray wrinkles or stray hairs. I played everything by the book. Eve just played.

I wanted to play too, to get invited to cool parties, to goof off with cute boys, to totally relax and have fun. I enjoyed babysitting every Saturday night, but it didn't make up for my sad social life.

I stroked my comforter, which always cheered

me up. Made of pretty lilac silk and embroidered with sweet ivory birds, my comforter was soft and beautiful. My parents had refused to pay for it, claiming it was overpriced and would get stained easily. They refused to pay for a lot of things. My mother worked with children in foster care. My father managed a food bank. In their spare time, they volunteered at a homeless shelter. Compared with the kids they saw every day, Eve and I had more than enough possessions. But Eve and I didn't see it that way. So I had bought my comforter with the money I'd earned babysitting. I cherished it. It wasn't the same as an invitation to a hot party. It wasn't even the next best thing to it. But it was mine.

I took my babysitting bag out of my closet and made sure I had everything I needed for tonight. Two educational board games: Check. Six library books to read to the children: Check. Rubber gloves for light housework after the children went to bed: Check. Checklist for the parents, specifying what the children did in their absence: Check.

I grabbed the bag and my cell phone—which hadn't cost much, but came with a pricey two-year service contract—and went outside to wait for my client . . .

To find out what happens, pick up

Kaitlyn
and the Competition